SELINA'S SUBMISSION

by

FRANCESCA LEWIS

CHIMERA

Selina's Submission first published in 1998 by
Chimera Publishing Ltd
PO Box 152
Waterlooville
Hants
PO8 9FS

Printed and bound in Great Britain by
Caledonian International Book Manufacturing Ltd
Glasgow

SELINA'S SUBMISSION

Francesca Lewis

Chapter One

As Oliver Richards drove smoothly along the winding Lincolnshire lanes he was acutely aware that Georgina was becoming increasingly restless. He glanced sideways at her.

'Not to your liking?' he asked with amusement.

'It's all flat and green,' said Georgina petulantly. 'I can't think why you were in such a rush to get up here.'

'Once I own something I like to put my mark on it,' said Oliver curtly.

Georgina shivered with excitement. 'But it's only a house,' she exclaimed.

'At the moment it's only a house,' he agreed.

Georgina crossed her long tanned legs, exposing a considerable expanse of thigh beneath the straight, short, oyster-coloured skirt that she was wearing teamed with a three quarter length navy buttoned jacket that had an oyster-coloured trim and side slits. No matter where she went Georgina always looked immaculate. 'I knew it,' she said delightedly. 'You're going to use this house that Hugh gambled away for training, aren't you?'

'The thought had crossed my mind,' admitted Oliver. It had more than crossed his mind, but at that stage he didn't intend to tell Georgina the full extent of his plans. She always played a leading role where Oliver and the training of his girlfriends were concerned, but since he had no one specific in mind at that moment there didn't seem any point in talking about it.

In fact, he was slightly irritated that the timing of his

win was so bad. He'd known for months now that eventually Hugh was going to go one step too far and gamble everything he had on the turn of a card. What he hadn't anticipated was that when it finally happened and he became the owner of Summerfield Hall he wouldn't have a new girlfriend ready to take there and train up.

'Every successful defence lawyer needs a country retreat,' he told Georgina.

'Agreed, but Lincolnshire!'

She sounded as though he was taking her to Blackpool, he thought, but then Georgina had never seen Summerfield Hall. He had, about a year ago when he'd had to drive Hugh home because he'd drunk too much. He'd decided then that he wanted to own it, and what Oliver Richards wanted, he always got in the end.

'Nearly there now,' he said briskly, turning the car sharply left as he saw a small signpost marked "Summerfield Village Only". About two hundred yards up what was little more than a dirt track Summerfield Hall came into view. He heard Georgina draw in her breath and smiled to himself. It was a very old, three-storey, early Victorian house, and although it was showing signs of decay the vast grounds were in excellent condition. It was clear that with a little money spent on it – and money presented no problem to Oliver – it could easily be restored to its early splendour.

Oliver remembered from his earlier visit that the front door was round the back of the house under an archway, and as he drew the car to a halt Georgina hugged her knees.

'You can almost imagine a coach and horses here, can't you?' she remarked.

'And all those serving wenches,' sighed Oliver.

'Yes, just think what a wonderful time you'd have had with them,' laughed Georgina.

'I don't know that it would have been quite the same,' mused Oliver, as he eased his long legs out of the car. 'The serving wenches had to say yes to everyone. They were, by their very occupation, used to servitude. It's far more fun to take a girl who isn't used to servitude and teach her the delights of submission.'

'Except that you never quite get what you want, do you?' said Georgina casually.

Oliver's mouth tightened ominously. He didn't need to be reminded about the last disaster. Lisette had been doing so well, he'd been certain that at last he'd found a girl he could train to the degree of submission he required, but she'd failed the final test and left him. He could still remember her, tears smudging her cheeks as she'd wrapped her naked abused body in a satin sheet and stared at him across the four-poster bed in his London house.

'I can't do it, Oliver,' she'd whispered, her eyes huge and frightened. 'This time you've asked too much of me.'

He'd let her go of course, that was always part of the agreement. They were all free to go whenever they wanted, but he'd been so certain that Lisette would do anything he demanded. Despite his anger at what he saw as her betrayal, he felt his penis stirring as he remembered the way she'd looked that final night, surrounded by all his friends, both male and female, her body twisting and turning in helpless ecstasy as she'd begged and beseeched them to let her shattered nerves rest.

'Hadn't you better ring the doorbell?' demanded Georgina sharply, and Oliver was snapped back to the present moment.

'It's gone midnight, do you think anyone will hear?'

'I hope so, after we've come all this way,' said Georgina irritably.

'You shouldn't frown so much,' Oliver told her. 'That

7

lovely smooth forehead of yours will suffer.'

'It's so kind of you to worry about me,' said Georgina dryly.

Oliver's mouth twitched in a slight smile. They both knew each other so well, which was fortunate because although he'd never admit it, Oliver needed Georgina. He had a wide circle of friends and acquaintances but out of all of them it was Georgina who understood his needs the best. Not by nature in the least submissive herself, she nevertheless took great delight in helping him whenever he was attempting a training session, and at times her inventiveness surprised even him.

They both heard the bell ringing, and in a surprisingly short space of time the front door was opened and someone, a deputy housekeeper Oliver assumed, stood in front of them.

Oliver automatically assessed her. She was about five foot five he supposed, and young, probably no more than nineteen. Despite the fact that she was wearing an incredibly ugly brown and beige checked shirt-dress that came down nearly to her ankles and was belted with what looked suspiciously like a plastic belt, there was no disguising the fact that she had an incredible figure. She was very full-breasted with a tiny waist, and a mass of tumbling chestnut hair framed a pale heart-shaped face from which large, trusting, dark eyes stared at him.

Oliver held out his hand. 'Good evening. I'm Oliver Richards, and...'

The girl's eyes became bewildered. 'I'm sorry, what did you say your name was?' she asked hesitantly.

'Oliver Richards,' he said crisply. 'I'm from London, and...'

'Has something happened to my father?' the girl asked anxiously.

8

Oliver turned to Georgina and raised his eyebrows. Georgina shrugged her slim shoulders and tapped her left foot impatiently on the cobbled stones.

'Who's your father?' Oliver demanded.

'Hugh Swift,' said the girl.

Oliver stared more intently at her. This was an unexpected surprise, and suddenly he wondered if she was going to be an even bigger prize than the house itself. There was something very unusual about her. She looked like a girl from another time, incredibly young, vulnerable and unsophisticated. He couldn't imagine how Hugh Swift had come to have such a daughter.

'I'd better come in,' he said firmly. 'I need to talk to you.'

The girl obeyed without hesitation, as though she was used to being commanded, and Oliver's pulse quickened.

'Did you know Hugh had a daughter?' he whispered to Georgina as the girl guided them through a darkened corridor and along a passageway into the main hall.

'Certainly not,' murmured Georgina. She paused for a moment. 'She's your type too,' she added with a sly grin.

'I couldn't be that lucky,' muttered Oliver, and then he and Georgina were ushered into the drawing room.

The furniture had clearly seen better days, but then so had everything in the room. Rather like Hugh, thought Oliver to himself.

'Won't you sit down,' said the girl nervously, and Oliver noticed that she had a very attractive voice. It was soft and pitched low. He hated women with strident voices. 'Are you a friend of my father's?' she asked.

'An acquaintance, certainly,' agreed Oliver, his eyes roaming from the girl's head to her feet and then back up to her face. Colour suffused her cheeks and she lowered her eyelids, and he noticed how long and dark her eyelashes were. 'What's your name?' he asked abruptly.

Her eyes flew open. 'I'm Selina,' she said, in some surprise. 'Surely you must know that, if you know my father?'

'I'm afraid he never mentioned you,' said Oliver, and the girl pouted and nibbled her lower lip.

'You must be wondering where your father is,' said Georgina kindly. Oliver smiled to himself. He could always rely on Georgina at awkward moments.

The girl nodded.

'I'm sorry to have to tell you this, Selina, but your father's been very stupid,' said Oliver briskly. He decided to swing into courtroom mode, it was the easiest way to dispense this kind of news. 'I'm sure you know that your father was addicted to gambling—'

'Gambling?' Selina's astonishment was evident.

Georgina gave a light laugh. 'Good heavens, yes! He was known all over London for it. What did you think he was doing when he was away from home?'

'I had no idea,' confessed Selina. 'He never talked about it, and naturally I didn't ask.'

'Why was that?' asked Oliver.

Selina's fingers rubbed nervously against the sides of her dress. 'He wouldn't have liked it,' she explained.

Oliver was becoming more and more aroused by the girl standing before him. She seemed so nervous and yet so anxious to please; a combination that would be irresistible if he ever got her into bed.

'Well, whether you knew it or not, it's true,' he continued, 'and I'm afraid that last night he gambled away this house and all its contents. Here's the document to prove it, in case my word isn't good enough for you.'

He could see that Selina's hand was trembling as she took the piece of paper from him and ran her eyes down the page.

'But, how could he do this?' she whispered.

'Only too easily, I'm afraid,' explained Oliver. 'Summerfield Hall was all he had left. He'd lost everything else on previous visits to London. Gambling was his only form of pleasure, Selina. He certainly didn't seem very interested in women.'

As he spoke he watched the girl closely, and once again the highly arousing flush tinted her cheeks.

'I wouldn't know anything about that,' she said quietly.

'Where will you go?' asked Georgina.

Suddenly Selina's legs seemed to give way, and she sank down into the large chair opposite Oliver's. 'I hadn't thought,' she said, in obvious horror. 'How could he do this? Are you sure he didn't mention me? Not at all?'

Oliver's mouth felt quite dry. He wondered what she was like in passion, if she even knew the meaning of such an emotion, that was. From the look of her he was beginning to think that the most excitement she would have experienced was a few hasty fumblings with some clumsy yokel's son from one of the nearby farms.

'I just don't know what to do,' she continued sadly. 'How could he do such a thing to us? And where is he – is he okay?'

Oliver found her instinctive concern for her rogue of a father, despite having just received the devastating news that she had lost her home thanks to his dubious gambling obsession, highly touching and incredibly arousing. She was staring at him with large doleful eyes as though expecting him to come up with a magical solution.

Oliver did indeed have a magical solution, but he decided to test the water very carefully. 'Yes, he's fine,' he assured her with a display of convincing sincerity. 'He's just gone away for a while to lick his wounds. But the important thing is you. Do you live here all the time, or are you at university?' he asked.

'Oh no, not university,' said Selina, and she gave him a shy smile, despite the evident sadness and confusion in her eyes. 'You see, my mother ran off years ago, when I was only five, and because of that my father's been very particular to keep me away from the temptations of the world. It's understandable; he must have been dreadfully hurt. But I'm sure I'm not like her.'

Oliver hoped she was, but it was clear that even if that were true Selina herself had no idea of it. 'So what have you been doing since you left school?' he continued, trying to sound interested despite his rising desire.

'I was educated at home until I was sixteen,' Selina explained. 'Since then I've spent my time here, acting as father's hostess and general housekeeper really.'

Georgina cleared her throat. 'It's been a very long drive from London, Selina,' she said sweetly. 'Do you think we could have a cup of coffee?'

Selina suddenly looked flustered and leapt to her feet. 'I'm so sorry,' she apologised meekly. 'What on earth must you think of me? Of course, I'll go and make some at once.'

As she hurried out of the room Georgina turned to Oliver and gave him a lazy smile. 'Are you thinking what I think you're thinking?' she purred.

Oliver nodded thoughtfully. 'I am, and I can't believe my luck,' he confessed, his heavy-lidded eyes gleaming with avaricious excitement. 'Old Hugh's been a bit of a dark horse. Fancy never mentioning he had such a beautiful creature for a daughter.'

'I know. She should have come gift-wrapped at Christmas for you,' said Georgina. 'And I wouldn't be surprised to find she's still a virgin.'

'No one's that lucky,' said Oliver, hoping he would be.

'Just the same, she's absolute perfection, and I'd love to see her without that ghastly dress on.'

'I'm sure you would,' murmured Georgina. 'I'd rather like to see her without that ghastly dress on as well. She's very eager to please, don't you think?'

'It looks as though Hugh trained her perfectly,' agreed Oliver. 'It's almost as though he knew my tastes.'

'He didn't, did he?' asked Georgina.

'Of course not. When did Hugh Swift ever discuss sex? No, this is just a slice of luck, too good to be wasted. And I'm going to make the most of it. Do you think I can persuade her to stay on?'

'It doesn't sound to me as though she's got anywhere else to go,' Georgina pointed out. 'Be careful, though. If you scare her off now you won't get any fun at all.'

'I don't need to be told how to start a seduction,' said Oliver, curtly. But he took her point. Selina was so special that he was going to have to be very careful indeed. Yet at the same time he had to make sure she understood what was going to be expected from her.

She came back in carrying a large silver tray with a matching silver coffee pot and three bone china cups on it. 'I brought cream and sugar, I hope that's all right?' she remarked, putting the tray down on a small sidetable.

'No sugar for me, thank you,' drawled Georgina. 'I have to keep an eye on my figure.'

Selina looked enviously at her. 'I wish I was slim like you,' she said admiringly. 'Father was always on at me about my weight.'

'I'm glad you didn't listen to him,' said Oliver. 'Most men like women to have some shape to them.'

'It's all right,' Georgina told Selina as the girl looked anxiously at her. 'I've known him for far too long to be insulted by his remarks. Besides, not all men share his tastes.'

Selina looked thoroughly flustered, and Oliver noticed her cup clatter nervously against the saucer as she tried to drink some of her coffee.

'I've been thinking about what's to become of you,' he said slowly, 'while you've been out of the room.'

'So have I,' confessed Selina. 'I realise you'll want me gone as soon as possible, but I just can't think where to go.'

'Maybe you won't have to leave after all.'

'What do you mean?' asked Selina, in obvious astonishment.

Oliver took a deep breath. If he handled this right then the next few weeks should prove some of the most sexually exciting of his life. 'You could always stay on as *my* hostess and housekeeper,' he said casually.

'But, you might like things done differently,' she said, hoping he wouldn't.

'I'm sure I will, and I ought to tell you at this point that I demand total obedience from everyone connected with me, whether it's in the office or in my home. Do I make myself clear?'

'Oh, yes.' Selina nodded eagerly. 'That's quite all right, I'm used to following rules. My father was very demanding, and everything always had to be just right for him.'

'Mm, but this might be slightly different,' murmured Oliver.

'I'm sure it'll be fine,' Selina assured him. 'As long as you tell me what it is you want, then I'll do it to the best of my ability.'

From the corner of his eye Oliver saw Georgina's head turn towards him, but he refused to meet her gaze. 'I'm very pleased to hear it,' he said softly, 'but you should be careful what you promise.'

Selina looked bewildered. 'I'm very trustworthy,' she said.

'You may not like some of my rules,' remarked Oliver, and he heard Georgina stifle a chuckle behind a sip of coffee.

'Why not?' queried Selina. 'After all, this is your house now.'

'There is one other thing you should know,' continued Oliver. 'If you ever feel uncomfortable with my rules, or I ask you to do something you don't want to do, then of course you'll be perfectly free to go.'

'I can't imagine that happening,' said Selina, in wide-eyed innocence. 'Besides, where would I go?'

'That's not the point,' said Oliver sharply. 'The point is I want you to understand that you're free to leave at any moment, but that if you choose to stay you must do everything I say.'

He could see she didn't understand him, and that only excited him more. He couldn't wait for the moment when she first began to realise what he was talking about, but for now it seemed wise to say nothing more.

'Of course I understand,' she said, smiling nervously at him. 'I hope I'll prove completely satisfactory to you.'

'So do I...' murmured Oliver, '...so do I. You have absolutely no idea how much I hope that.'

'I'm so relieved,' said Selina, glancing from Oliver to Georgina with a cheerful expression on her face. 'I know it's a dreadful thing that my father's done, and of course I'll miss him terribly, but at least thanks to you I won't be homeless. I'm not really trained to do anything else but work here.'

'Oliver will soon change that,' said Georgina. Oliver glared at her, but she just smiled mischievously at him. Luckily for Oliver, Selina didn't pick up on the remark.

'Did you want to stay overnight?' she asked them.

'We've driven all this way,' said Georgina. 'We're hardly likely to return to London at this time, now are we?'

'No, of course not, that was stupid of me,' the girl apologised hurriedly.

'Then prepare two bedrooms for us before you retire for the night,' said Oliver curtly. 'As from now, I'm the master of Summerfield Hall.'

Chapter Two

As was usual, Selina's alarm went off at seven a.m., but whereas she was normally quick to jump out of bed, today her body felt heavy and her head ached. Despite her show of courage the previous evening, she'd been left devastated at her father's betrayal. Although Oliver Richards had offered her an opportunity to stay on in her own home, she felt very anxious about his terms and conditions. She knew she was unworldly, her father had made certain of that, but even so she'd sensed something strange about the tall dark barrister who'd arrived so unexpectedly.

The relationship between him and the slim, elegant Georgina was puzzling too. Selina thought Georgina incredibly attractive, and had definitely sensed sexual undercurrents between her and Oliver. Despite that the pair had requested separate bedrooms, and that both puzzled and disturbed Selina. She wondered what their relationship really was, and wondered too how she fitted into Oliver's plans for the future.

Realising that she had no idea whether he ate breakfast or not, she quickly pulled on her everyday clothes. In the summer these consisted of a long loose skirt and short-sleeved cotton jumper, with the almost compulsory strand of pearls that had been her father's present to her on her eighteenth birthday. Despite the fact that it was mid-June, Summerfield Hall was always cold, and it was only when she went outside that she was able to wear summer clothing. As she pulled on her sensible cream court shoes there was a light tap on her door and she froze for an instant, every instinct telling her that it was Oliver standing outside on the landing.

'Yes?' she asked nervously.

'It's Georgina,' called the other woman. 'I've a message for you from Oliver. He won't be taking breakfast this morning, but he'd like to see you in the drawing room in half an hour, before he leaves for London.'

'Would you like anything?' Selina asked, opening her bedroom door slightly.

Georgina, dressed more casually in a loose, light beige trouser suit with a cream camisole tunic underneath the jacket, smiled warmly at Selina, but for some reason the smile didn't reassure the girl. 'Coffee will do me fine, thank you,' she said lightly, 'and I can easily make that for myself. Just don't be late for your meeting with Oliver, will you? He's a stickler for punctuality.'

When Selina walked into the drawing room, exactly on time, she saw Oliver glance at his watch and then nod in approval. This morning he looked very stern, and there was something about the expression in his eyes that made Selina feel both nervous and excited at the same time. His eyes swept over her, and her flesh tingled like it did when she sometimes allowed her own hands to roam over her flesh beneath the bedclothes at night. She knew that was wrong, but often she couldn't help herself, and many times she'd wondered what it would be like to have a man's hands replace her own. Suddenly, the prospect of Oliver being that man was terrifying.

'Since I'm returning to London,' he said briskly, 'I think that perhaps we should have a proper interview, don't you? After all, I really know nothing about you except that you're Hugh's daughter, and that hardly counts as a recommendation.'

Selina's heart plummeted. Was she to be made jobless

18

and homeless after all? 'I… I can't give you any references,' she stammered. 'As I explained last night, I've only ever worked for my father.'

'I'm a very good judge of people,' Oliver assured her. 'Particularly women.' As he spoke Selina realised that Georgina had come into the room, and was standing in front of the door as though blocking the exit. 'Now, take off those dreadful clothes,' said Oliver suddenly.

Selina couldn't believe that she'd heard him correctly. 'You – you want me to go and change?'

He gave a harsh laugh. 'Hardly. I want you to undress here, in front of me.'

Selina shook her head in disbelief. 'I – I couldn't possibly do that. You want me to be your housekeeper, don't you? I mean...'

'Fine,' Oliver sounded totally bored. 'Then I suggest you pack and leave immediately. Clearly you didn't take in what I said about total obedience.'

Selina had never felt so utterly alone in her whole life. What on earth was going on? She stared at Oliver and he gazed back at her, his eyes totally indifferent to her confusion. Then she glanced at Georgina, who nodded encouragingly at her. To her amazement, Selina realised that her nipples had hardened, and she could feel them brushing against her cotton bra. She couldn't believe it was happening, not at such a humiliating moment, but there was no denying the physical evidence.

'It was nice to meet you,' said Oliver, turning away dismissively. 'Now if you don't mind…'

Selina was desperate. 'I – I'm sorry,' she blurted, attempting to retrieve the situation.

Oliver turned back to her, a gleam of interest in his eyes. 'You mean, you'll do as I say?'

Selina hesitated for a moment, trying to make sense of

her swirling emotions, and then bowed her head and nodded miserably. Her fingers started to fumble awkwardly with the zip at the side of her skirt.

As she stepped out of it Oliver turned to Georgina. 'For God's sake get her some new clothes before I get back from London,' he snapped impatiently. 'I never want to see her dressed like this again, do you understand?'

'I think I know your taste well enough,' Georgina assured him.

Selina was down to her cotton bra and panties. She had stepped out of her court shoes. For a long moment Oliver simply stood and looked at her. 'Take off her bra,' he eventually said to Georgina.

'I can do it myself,' protested Selina.

'Dear me,' he said heavily. 'You really do have trouble obeying orders, don't you Selina? If I'd wanted you to remove your own bra I'd have asked you to.'

Selina bit her lip and backed nervously away as Georgina advanced upon her, but the woman swiftly put an arm around her slender waist and halted her retreat. Then Selina felt her bra being unclipped and Georgina removed it with a deft expertise. 'Now be a good girl and stand quietly for him,' Georgina whispered in her ear, and this time Selina didn't dare protest.

She longed to fold her arms across her naked breasts to conceal them from the man's penetrating gaze, but she knew such coyness would be forbidden. Already she was beginning to grasp the intricacies of her indoctrination which, she realised with increasing terror, was only just beginning.

Oliver took two steps towards her and then, almost idly, he reached out with both hands and pinched her aching nipples. At first the pressure was very light, and she felt a wave of pleasure wash through her. But then the pressure increased, and kept increasing until pain seared through her breasts and she gave a low moan of distress.

Suddenly Oliver released her and stepped back, his eyes gauging the extent of her arousal. Slowly the pain ebbed away, and Selina was both astonished and humiliated to realise that she was damp between her thighs.

'Interesting,' mused Oliver, thoughtfully. 'It seems you may have a taste for this kind of thing. How many men have you known, Selina?'

She didn't fully understand the question. 'Not many,' she confessed. 'And most of those are my father's age.'

Georgina laughed. 'He meant *sexually*, darling,' she drawled seductively.

Selina was mortified by the suggestion and embarrassed by her stupid naïvety. 'N-none,' she whispered.

Oliver raised an eyebrow, glanced at Georgina, and then back at the hapless girl. 'I find that very hard to believe. I hope you wouldn't lie to me, my dear.'

Selina shook her head, and as she did so she was acutely aware that her breasts swayed gently. 'Of course not,' she whispered. 'I wouldn't lie to anyone.'

'That's encouraging,' said Oliver. 'Well, we're going to have an interesting time over the next few weeks, Selina.'

As she tried to absorb his meaning she was barely aware of him moving in again. But her breathing grew a little more rapid as he ran his hands down her flanks. He lingered for a moment over the delicate flare of her hips, before running his fingers down over her white cotton panties, and then between her thighs, where he discovered the tell-tale signs of her arousal. 'Yes, I was right about you,' he said, with obvious satisfaction. 'Now, stand with your feet slightly apart.'

Selina did as she was told, and felt one of his knowing fingers lightly touch her sex through the thin material of her panties. Then she gasped as the finger abruptly stabbed upwards and she felt her sex lips part as the cotton was pushed between them. Her legs weakened when he flicked casually against the nub of her clitoris, that was emerging from its protective hood as her excitement grew still further.

Selina had never felt such sensations. Her breasts seemed to swell, and there was a heat between her thighs that was spreading inexorably upwards through her belly. She longed for something more, without fully understanding what.

Oliver watched with interest as the pink flush of desire began to appear on her breasts and chest, and he saw how her legs were shaking as she stood with them slightly parted as he'd ordered. When he touched her clitoris her head rocked back slightly and the breath snagged in her throat, but it was clear from the bewildered look in her eyes that she still didn't understand what was happening to her.

'That will do for now,' he said abruptly, withdrawing his finger and moving away from the confused and trembling girl.

Selina felt desolate. She didn't want him to leave her like that, desperately yearning for something – something that was so near, and yet so far. But there was nothing she could do about it, so she simply stood there, flushed and flustered, as Georgina and Oliver watched her with unconcealed amusement.

'I shall be away for about two days,' Oliver told her as she continued to stand with her feet apart, horribly aware of the way her panties were still moulded into her over-excited sex, but not daring to move until given permission. 'While I'm away Georgina will get things organised here, so that when I return we'll really be able to get started on training you to my ways. Of course, in time I shall be doing a lot of entertaining, but I don't think you're quite ready for that yet.'

'I… I am used to entertaining,' Selina said quietly. 'My father often held dinner parties here.'

'But I doubt they were like my dinner parties, or that you've previously played the kind of role I intend you to play,' Oliver replied, and suddenly Selina realised that this wasn't simply a demonstration of his power over her. He intended to use her sexually in any way he liked, and not only that, to let his guests use her as well.

She looked at Georgina in the vain hope of finding some support. 'He doesn't mean what I think he means, does he?' she asked tremulously.

'Probably,' said Georgina, with a smile. 'Don't worry, you can always leave – remember?'

The great problem was, Selina didn't really want to go anywhere. She'd always wondered about the mysteries of sex, but she was terrified that if this enigmatic man had his way, then she might turn out to be more like her mother than she wanted to be, and that thought was more than she could bear. Her father had told her so often that her mother had been a disgrace to her own sex, and that ladies didn't take lovers or allow themselves to be led astray by the delights of the flesh. And yet here she was taking pleasure from being intimately touched by a total stranger. Even now her body was yearning for him to touch her again. She felt so guilty, but what could she do? She had nowhere else to go, and he was already exerting a strange power over her that she felt helpless to resist.

'Is there anything special I should do for your return?' she asked.

'No, Georgina will see that everything is to my liking. Now you can go and get dressed.' He dismissively pointed at the discarded clothes on the floor. 'But put on something more exciting than those rags.'

'I don't have that many clothes to choose from,' Selina confessed sadly.

'Then walk around in your underwear,' said Oliver irritably. 'Anything's preferable to that dreadful jumper and skirt. Which reminds me,' he added thoughtfully, 'is there any way we can get this place heated? Life will be so much more pleasant for all of us if the rooms are warm.'

'I can get the fires lit,' Selina assured him.

'Get a man in to do it,' said Oliver. 'While I'm gone Georgina will keep you far too busy to be lugging coal around.' He turned to the blonde. 'If you decide more domestics are needed just ring me and I'll send some of my staff up from London. What I want you to do is to get Selina's wardrobe sorted out, and to arrange a quiet little dinner for just the two of us on the evening of my return.'

Georgina pouted. 'And what about me?'

'I'll bring you something to play with, shall I?'

Georgina smiled again. 'That would be nice,' she said lightly, and the pair of them exchanged a glance of complicity.

Oliver was seen off by Georgina, and Selina hurried up to her bedroom determined to find something, anything, to wear. She certainly had no intention of walking around the house in her underwear for all the staff to see!

'And what are you doing?'

Selina spun round and saw the elegant blonde standing in the open doorway, one hand on the ornate handle. 'I'm… I'm just looking for something to wear,' she explained. She was well aware that while Oliver was away Georgina was his representative in the house, and as such she had to be respected and obeyed.

'I'll help you,' said the beautiful woman. 'And I think it's time you and I had a little chat, don't you?'

'If you like,' Selina conceded meekly, having a fair idea

24

of what the chat might be about.

'I do like,' Georgina said abruptly. 'Now, I'll explain things a little more clearly for you, as you don't seem to have quite grasped it all yet.'

She paused until it was clear she had Selina's fullest attention.

'You probably don't realise it yet,' she eventually continued, 'but your father did you a great favour when he gambled away Summerfield Hall. You're going to have the most exciting summer of your life.'

Selina wondered how it was that the woman managed to make that sound more like a threat than a promise.

Georgina busily rummaged through Selina's drawers, and then held up two more cotton bras and several pairs of white cotton panties. 'Don't you have any fancy underwear?' she asked.

'Well no, that's perfectly practical,' explained Selina.

'But it's not at all what Oliver will want,' said Georgina firmly. 'I can see I'm going to have to fit you out with everything, even the basics.'

'Does it really matter what I wear while he's away?' asked Selina, a little hesitantly.

Georgina shrugged. 'I suppose not; wear what's comfortable. He'll be back soon enough, and then everything will change.'

Selina sat on the edge of her bed. For some reason the jumper and skirt she'd worn earlier no longer held any appeal, and as she tried to decide what she should wear instead, she was very aware that the other woman was watching her closely.

Suddenly Georgina sat down on the bed next to her and ran one immaculately manicured fingernail down Selina's right thigh, leaving a small red line in its wake. 'You have the most wonderful pale skin,' she said huskily. 'And it

25

marks so easily, too. How divine!'

Selina shivered, for there was no mistaking the cruelty behind the woman's words. 'I – I want to get dressed now, please,' she blustered hastily.

'Don't worry,' cooed Georgina. 'I'm not allowed to touch you… not yet, anyway.'

Selina felt her body tighten with trepidation. 'Yet?' she whispered.

'Once Oliver's introduced you to some of the more, shall we say – conservative – sexual practices, he'll start to broaden your horizons, and that's where I come in.'

'I thought I was to be a housekeeper and hostess,' protested Selina, wondering why it was that despite her fear, moisture was once again escaping from between her sex lips and dampening the cotton of her panties.

'A euphemism,' said Georgina swiftly. 'There's something you ought to know about Oliver. He may be one of the country's most successful defence lawyers and incredibly rich, but he's still searching for his perfect woman. His main hobby is trying to track down this elusive creature, but so far he's had no success.'

'But I don't see what that's got to do with me,' said Selina, feeling totally bewildered.

'Surely you can't be that naïve,' said Georgina scornfully, idly running her fingers through Selina's hair, and then hastily snatching them away as though remembering that the girl was out of bounds. 'Surely you realise Oliver's interested in you… sexually.'

'But… but I've no experience with men,' protested Selina.

'Exactly!' purred Georgina. 'That's why he's so excited. You see, Oliver wants to train a girl to become his ideal woman, and that's quite difficult because most girls these days have very strong ideas of what they do and don't want

– in bed, that is. For you everything will be new, and he's intending to mould you to fit his desires.'

Selina's eyes widened with shock. 'I'm not sure I want to be moulded to fit his desires,' she protested.

'Don't worry,' Georgina said softly. 'You're a very sensual girl, it's just that you're totally inexperienced. Oliver will soon change all that.'

Selina was staggered by what she was hearing, and yet she was also fascinated both by the prospect of feeling Oliver's hands on her in what she fondly imagined would be gentle sexual caresses, and by the realisation that her body was anxious to learn.

'If we stay here much longer I won't be able to resist you myself,' said Georgina suddenly. 'For goodness sake, cover yourself up and show me around the house. I need to see how many rooms there are and decide what uses Oliver can put them to. I'll meet you downstairs once you're dressed.'

Somewhat surprised by the other woman's behaviour, Selina nevertheless obeyed, and within ten minutes she was taking the elegant blonde on a detailed tour of Summerfield Hall. To her surprise, Georgina didn't seem interested in the beautiful architecture, or the well-stocked library, or the beautifully furnished dining room. But when she heard that to get to the oldest wing of the house it was necessary to cross a small stone bridge she became quite excited and demanded that Selina took her there immediately.

'We haven't used the wing very much,' explained Selina as they crossed the old arch and walked through a creaking wooden door into a rather damp smelling room. 'As you can see, it's pretty unlived-in.'

'What exactly is there here?' asked Georgina.

'Well, there's a kind of a playroom, with a sort of cellar underneath.'

'A playroom?' Georgina's blue eyes glinted. 'What fun! Do tell, what games do you play there?'

Selina felt very uncomfortable. 'I've never played anything there,' she confessed. 'It's just a room. It's always been known as the playroom, but it's never been used as such.'

'Well it will be now,' said Georgina firmly. 'It's an ideal room for Oliver to stock all his toys in,' and she laughed to herself. 'Now, you must show me this cellar.'

Sighing, Selina opened the door leading to some rickety steps down into the cellar. 'Mind how you go, it's easy to fall,' she warned the other woman as they descended carefully.

Georgina shivered. 'My, it's cold down here.'

'It's supposed to be. I think wine should be stored here, only my father drank all of his before it got this far.'

Selina felt for the switch, and to her surprise the light still worked. She watched as Georgina looked around in obvious delight. 'Look at that low beam,' she enthused. 'How absolutely perfect.'

'For what?' asked Selina.

Georgina looked at her in surprise for a moment, and then clapped her hands together. 'You are so naïve it's an absolute delight to be with you.' Selina frowned at the comment. 'You mustn't worry about anything,' Georgina said swiftly. 'It's just that I know Oliver will adore this room.'

'You mean, he's a wine buff?' asked Selina.

'No, but he's very into dungeons,' said Georgina.

Selina had no idea what the woman was talking about. 'Do you want to see any more?' she asked warily, wanting to change the subject.

'No, this is absolutely perfect,' declared Georgina. 'Oliver will be thrilled when I tell him about it. He certainly didn't have any idea there was an even older wing to the house, let alone that it had a playroom and a dungeon.'

'It isn't a dungeon,' Selina protested stubbornly. 'It's a cellar.'

'Easily convertible,' Georgina assured her.

'Why would anyone want a dungeon these days?' asked Selina innocently.

'Let's go back to the main house,' said Georgina. 'I think I've seen enough now.'

After the tour of inspection that had clearly delighted Georgina, she drove off in Selina's car to the nearest town to buy the various clothes and accessories she seemed to feel it would be necessary for Selina to have before Oliver's return.

Left alone, Selina wandered aimlessly around the house. It had always been her home, so familiar and safe, but it didn't seem so familiar any more, and she certainly didn't feel safe. In fact, she almost felt as though she was a prisoner in her own home, which was totally ridiculous because, as Oliver had kept telling her, she was free to go whenever she wished. She cursed her father and his stupidity, but wished he was there to help her.

The next two days sped by as Georgina got Selina to organise a thorough cleaning and airing of the whole house. Fresh drapes and furnishings were brought in, while everything that was left was polished and spring-cleaned until it shone in a way Selina could never recall it shining before.

While all this was being done, Georgina seemed to spend most of her time in the old wing, and Selina often saw vans using the side entrance to deliver things. But she couldn't imagine what on earth Georgina needed or was doing to the playroom and the cellar.

Finally everything was to Georgina's satisfaction, and exactly four days later on the Friday after she first set eyes on him, Selina found herself standing in her bedroom waiting for Georgina to come and tell her how she was to dress for Oliver's first evening in residence as master of Summerfield Hall.

Selina stood outside the dining room and glanced anxiously at Georgina. 'These clothes feel all wrong,' she whispered. 'I'm supposed to be his housekeeper.'

'Not tonight,' said Georgina with a half smile. 'Tonight you're his hostess. Anyway, he'll adore your dress.'

Selina wasn't sure Georgina was right. The dress was ivory-coloured with a strapless bodice that fitted tightly over her voluptuous breasts and clung to her like a second skin, emphasising her tiny waist and softly rounded hips. It ended a couple of inches above her knees, and she had a white sash tied around her waist. She felt like some virgin in ancient times about to be sacrificed to a demanding god, and started to tremble. Georgina pushed open the door before Selina could argue any further, and guided the girl into the room.

Oliver looked immaculate in a dark pinstripe suit, white shirt and red and blue striped tie. Standing next to him was a tiny Oriental girl wearing a Chinese style dress with a high mandarin collar. She had beautiful straight black hair, and she looked as uncertain as Selina felt.

'My toy!' exclaimed Georgina, rushing across the room and flinging her arms round Oliver's neck. She kissed him lightly on the cheek and he smiled at her.

'I hope you like her,' he said. 'She should suit you very well, from what I hear.'

'Wonderful!' enthused Georgina, and as Selina watched in astonishment she grasped the timid girl by the wrist and pulled her out of the room. The girl made no sound of protest, but as she passed Selina she looked at her with an expression of such terrified appeal on her face that Selina wondered what on earth was going to happen to her.

'Alone at last,' said Oliver quietly.

Immediately Selina's thoughts returned to what was going to happen to her. Nervously nibbling her lower lip she gave him a wan smile. 'I hope everything's to your liking,' she murmured politely.

'From what I've seen so far you and Georgina have done an excellent job,' he assured her. 'Would you care for a drink?'

Selina nodded, but before she could say what she wanted he'd handed her a glass of red wine. 'To the future,' he said, raising his glass.

'To the future,' echoed Selina, even though she was unsure of what that future held.

'Before we begin our intimate dinner,' continued Oliver, 'you do remember the terms and conditions of your employment here, I trust?' Selina nodded. 'Excellent, then we can start.'

Selina glanced at the table. It was laid for a meal, and she wondered if she should ring for some food. 'We'll eat later,' said Oliver, clearly guessing what was going through her mind. 'I find I always have an appetite afterwards...'

Suddenly Selina felt very frightened, and without realising it she started to back nervously towards the door.

'Come over here,' Oliver instructed her, the tone of his voice leaving her in no doubt that if she disobeyed their agreement would be over before it had even begun. Slowly, as though hypnotised, she moved towards him. He nodded, but without any trace of a smile to soften the harshness of his features; a harshness she hadn't really noticed on his previous visit. 'The dress is perfect,' he complimented her.

'Georgina chose it,' admitted Selina.

'I guessed that,' he remarked, 'but it still suits you.' Suddenly he reached behind her and undid the white sash, trailing it over her bare shoulders as he drew it into his hands.

'Yes,' he said speculatively, 'that's better. Now turn around.'

Selina did as she was told. For a moment his fingers touched the bare skin of her shoulders, and then to her astonishment he tugged at the zip on the back of the dress and without a word spun her back to face him and peeled it off her. He wasn't gentle. Suddenly the dress was lying around her ankles, and she was left standing in her white high-heeled sandals, matching white hold-up stockings, and the white G-string with the lacy front that Georgina had insisted she wore.

Oliver studied her closely. 'You really are delicious,' he said thoughtfully. 'If only I'd known about you sooner, I'd have made sure we played cards for Summerfield Hall a long time ago.' Then taking her hand, he moved across the room and sat her down on the edge of the chaise longue, before kneeling in front of her and slowly running his hands up and down her arms.

Selina's skin prickled and tiny currents of electricity seemed to run from her arms to her breasts. She felt hot and flustered.

Oliver kept his unfathomable dark eyes fixed on her face as he very slowly and tenderly trailed his fingertips across her collarbone and down over the tops of her breasts until his fingers were resting lightly, teasingly, on her rapidly hardening nipples.

'You know what I'm going to do next, don't you?' he murmured.

Selina suddenly remembered the searing pain of his

previous caress and she shrank away from him, trying to press her body into the back of the chaise longue.

'Sit still,' he commanded. And then, with cruel deliberation, he pinched the amazingly sensitive nipples until once more her nerve-endings screamed in protest and she gave a tiny whimper. But even as she did so she felt a strange dark pleasure coursing through her tender breasts; a pleasure that almost, but not quite, managed to override the pain.

Oliver kept his fingers tightly on the protruding buds until Selina was certain she could bear it no longer. Then he abruptly released them, and bending forward, drew the tip of his tongue across the throbbing flesh.

'You enjoyed that,' he whispered. 'There's no use denying it, your body betrays you,' and even as he spoke he was sliding a hand down over her gently rounded belly, and his fingers dipped beneath the elastic of her panties and were travelling through her crisp dark pubic hair and probing between her sex lips. With tantalising slowness he drew lazy circles around the damp tissue between her swelling labia, and when he brushed against her clitoris Selina gasped with surprise as a searing sensation that was totally new to her shot through her belly. She stared at him with a mixture of fear and desire.

Oliver stood up and gazed down at her thoughtfully. The moment he withdrew his hand Selina felt bereft, and was shocked at her wanton behaviour. 'I shouldn't be doing this,' she whimpered, looking up at him anxiously. 'It's wrong.'

'Then tell me to stop. Tell me you want to go.'

But she didn't, because her whole body was so aching with need that she knew she couldn't possibly leave now.

Reaching down Oliver pulled her to her feet again, and before she knew what was happening he wrenched her arms roughly behind her back and quickly fastened her wrists with the sash from her dress. Her full breasts were thrust even further forward, and tiny blue veins showed faintly through the alabaster flesh.

Her nipples throbbed, and she longed to feel his tongue on them again, but it was clear that Oliver had other intentions. He pushed her back onto the chaise longue. She fell full length, and in one swift movement he knelt beside her, and then with alarming roughness he hooked his fingers into her panties and ripped them apart.

His sudden animalistic intensity shocked and frightened her.

'Please, please don't hurt me,' she begged. But Oliver ignored her. He stroked her inner thighs with surprising gentleness, and then in total contrast he pushed them roughly apart, and she realised she was lying naked except for her stockings, totally exposed to his merciless gaze.

Oliver crouched so that his head was between Selina's legs, and then he grasped her buttocks with both hands, lifting her so he could cover her moist vulva with his mouth. And then his tongue was invading her, swirling around her frantic clitoris and thrusting deep into her virginal vagina as she squirmed and writhed helpless and panic-stricken beneath him.

Oliver was very strong, and there was nothing Selina could do to stop the hideously enchanting sensations that were engulfing her. She felt a strange coiling sensation deep within her belly and her muscles started to quake and tighten. She cried out in panic, but Oliver simply gripped her buttocks even harder. He closed his mouth around the nub of her pleasure, swirled his tongue over the tip, and at the same time thrust two fingers into her aching channel.

His cruel yet clever fingers swiftly located a tiny spot that nearly sent Selina into a frenzy as even more nerve-endings began to tighten in anticipation of her first climax. Her body, so long deprived of any sensual stimulation, felt as though it was about to burst. She barely noticed the uncomfortable ache in her pinned arms. Tears misted her eyes as he reached up and alternately pinched her pulsating nipples. Then, as his tongue continued its cunning manipulations, all the extraordinary sensations that had been building up suddenly came together in one incredible explosion, and Selina's head jerked back into the cushions as she cried out in disbelief at the wonderful moment of piercing pleasure and relief.

When it was over she collapsed limply, her breathing ragged. Oliver stared down at her as she lay there totally dishevelled, flushed and incredibly beautiful. He hastily removed his clothes. Selina watched him through half closed eyes, and then averted her gaze at the last moment, too timid to gaze upon the erection she knew he would have. When naked, Oliver slid a tiny copper ring from a pocket of his discarded trousers. 'Open your legs,' he said curtly.

Selina's body was so sensitive, especially between her thighs, that she automatically clenched them tightly together at his words.

'Didn't you hear what I said?' he snapped.

But still she couldn't bring herself to obey, and to her shock and disbelief he swooped down like a ruthless vulture and she felt his teeth close around her left nipple, and pain such as she'd never experienced before tore through her.

'Why… why do you keep hurting me?' she whimpered pitifully.

'Hurting you?' he said softly as his teeth released the abused nipple. 'It's a special kind of pleasure I'm providing, but then you already know that, don't you? You suit me, Selina. You're a very special person.'

'No, I'm not,' she protested, because she didn't want to be. But she had the dreadful suspicion that he was right, otherwise why was she still lying there allowing him to do such things to her?

He ignored her denial. 'Now, will you open your legs for me, or do I have to punish you again?' he asked.

Totally confused, Selina did as she was told, and waited tensely as she felt his fingers moving between her thighs, dipping into the moisture that was seeping from her and stroking it upwards over the sensitive flesh that had so recently been pleasured. She felt too tender and made a sound of protest, but Oliver glared at her, and after that she remained silent.

With a twisted smile Oliver carefully eased back the hood of flesh that was protecting her clitoris. Once fully exposed he slid the tiny copper ring over it, and then tightened the ring until her clitoris was standing fully erect, trapped, and the hood could no longer protect it. Now he was able to tease it remorselessly, constantly flicking and licking at the tiny bud that could give such agony and ecstasy according to how he used it.

Selina felt certain that she wouldn't be able to bear it as he relentlessly aroused her. A tiny sigh escaped her as he lightly drew the tip of one finger across the trapped nub. But even as he did so her treacherous body started to melt and flickers of excitement spread so that she rolled her head restlessly from side to side, and once more that strange sensation stirred in her belly.

'You're going to come again, aren't you?' said Oliver.

'I don't know,' cried Selina, her upper body twisting restlessly on her aching arms.

'Well I know,' he said confidently. 'I can tell,' and he moved his free hand onto her abdomen and began to stroke very lightly. But slowly the caress turned into a massage, and he pressed firmly on the muscles that were already contracting and tightening in preparation for another climax.

Selina felt faint as the glorious sensations started to build again. The strange tingling in her toes that had preceded her first climax returned, and her fingers clenched, her nails digging into her palms as she reached the very edge and then, shockingly, Oliver stopped all stimulation and stood up.

Selina's eyes had been closed, but they flew open and she saw he was looking down at her. 'Beg me for it,' he said calmly.

Selina shook her head. 'I can't,' she protested.

'Then you won't be able to come, will you?' he taunted cruelly, his eyes absorbing her over-excited body. 'I can keep you like this for as long as I want, you know. Unless you beg me now we'll just end the evening here.'

Selina couldn't bear the cruel torture. 'Please... please...' she whispered, ashamed of her own weakness.

'Please what?' he teased.

'I don't know,' she sobbed, wishing she could cover her face with her hands. 'I don't know what to say.'

'Beg me to let you come,' he prompted.

Selina began to cry quietly, tears rolling down her face. 'Please... please let me come,' she whimpered, and immediately Oliver knelt between her thighs again. Once more his tongue moved in lazy circles around the trapped clitoris while his hands massaged her aching breasts and belly, until she was shaken by a second beautiful orgasm.

As she tried to recover Oliver looked thoughtfully at her. 'I think we'll do that one more time,' he said slowly.

'No...' she protested weakly. 'I can't bear it, really, I've had enough. You're hurting me.'

'But you like the pain,' said Oliver, and before she could answer him she felt his fingers moving inside her. But he was thrusting more urgently now, and for the first time he lowered his naked body onto hers, and she felt the touch of his erection. Then he moved the tip of his glans over her trapped clitoris, and although her flesh shrank from the contact he continued with deliberate cruelty, and eventually forced yet another shattering climax from her sorely abused body.

This time when she was finally still Oliver drew away for a brief moment, and then she felt the tip of his cock pressing against her opening, and even as she gave a muffled protest he thrust violently into her. He totally disregarded the fact that he was the first man ever to possess her, and even as she cried out with the pain of it he was moving rapidly and rhythmically, and as his excitement mounted, so did hers.

At last he allowed himself his own pleasure, and while he moved Selina gazed up at him and uttered a mewing cry of pleasure as once more the waves of a climax crashed down on her. She felt him stiffen and heard him gasp, and then she was being filled with his hot sperm, and when he withdrew she felt it trickle on her inner thighs as she lay in an abandoned heap, aching and totally confused by everything that had happened to her.

Oliver removed the ring that had trapped her clitoris and looked dispassionately down at her. 'I wonder what your father would think of you now,' he said as he rolled her a little to one side and untied the sash that bound her wrists, and the calculated cruelty of his words brought tears to her eyes. 'Don't bother to get dressed,' he continued dismissively. 'I think I shall eat alone. You can go to your room. No doubt you need some sleep.'

Selina stumbled to her feet, grabbed her clothing, and staggered out of the room. As she reached the bottom of the stairs she heard a feeble cry from the drawing room, swiftly followed by Georgina's harsh voice, and she fled to her room wondering what dreadful torments were being inflicted upon the poor Oriental girl.

And she wondered, too, what was in store for her in the days and weeks that lay ahead.

Chapter Three

'How was your evening, Oliver?' asked Georgina as she sat opposite him for breakfast the following morning.

He looked thoughtful for a moment. 'It went very well,' he said eventually. 'In fact, even better than I'd expected. There's a distinct possibility that little Selina is going to prove quite a prize. She doesn't realise it yet, but she has a natural aptitude for this kind of thing.'

'Really?' Georgina sounded excited, and Oliver shook his head reprovingly.

'Not yet, Georgina,' he said firmly. 'For the time being you can watch, but you cannot touch. There are several more things I have to teach the dear girl before anyone else is allowed to share in her fully.'

'Don't worry, I'll wait until I'm given permission,' she smiled. 'Anyway, I have to go back to London tomorrow night. I've had too much time away from the office already. I may be a partner now, but there are plenty of eager solicitors only too willing to step into my shoes if I stay away for too long.'

'I've taken some leave,' said Oliver.

Georgina was shocked. Oliver never took leave. He was a man who hated to be idle, and loved his work with a passion. Sex was his only diversion, but never before had he taken leave in order to indulge himself. He *must* have special plans for Selina.

'I'd like to be here for a couple of weeks to get the dear girl started properly,' he continued. 'I've a very special feeling about this one, Georgina, and I don't want to risk letting her slip away. She just could be the one.'

'Mm, I've heard that before,' said Georgina doubtfully.

Oliver frowned at her. 'Are you suggesting that I don't know what I'm doing?'

'Of course not,' she said hastily. She knew better than to antagonise Oliver. Her life was more complicated than his. As a dominant bisexual there were times when their paths hardly ever crossed, but he was able to supply her with submissive girls whenever she wanted, and his dinner parties were so select that to be crossed off his list of guests was a fate too hideous to contemplate.

'That's good,' he said flatly. 'I'd hate for us to fall out over Selina.'

'I had a very agreeable time last night, too,' she said, hoping to change the subject.

Oliver gave her one of his rare smiles. 'I thought you would. She came very highly recommended, if you know what I mean.'

'Where did you get her from?' Georgina enquired. 'She's been wonderfully well trained.'

'A friend of mine,' said Oliver vaguely. 'She tired of her though, and asked me if I knew anyone who might like to take her on.'

'Tired of her?' Georgina thought for a moment. 'I suppose her pain threshold is rather low, but she's incredibly skilful, and drove me to such delicious delight.' She shivered a little as she remembered the wicked fun of the previous night. 'Besides which, she cries beautifully. Her name's Kim, did you know?'

'I never thought to ask,' said Oliver indifferently. 'And what do you intend to do with Kim when you return to London?'

'I don't know,' confessed Georgina. 'I'd really like to keep her here. It would be a shame to have someone spoil her while I'm working, and you know what some people are like.'

'She should be safe enough here,' said Oliver, agreeably. 'She might be useful as well. Which reminds me,' he added, 'I'd like my London staff sent here for the next couple of weeks. I shall have the local people removed from the house. It will be easier to train Selina if she's surrounded by strangers.'

'Who do you need?' the beautiful woman asked.

'My housekeeper, my handyman, and my maid,' said Oliver. 'I expect Selina will object when I tell her she's to get rid of her employees, but since I now own Summerfield Hall, the choice isn't hers to make.'

'And what do you have planned for the rest of the weekend?' asked Georgina.

'You'll see,' said Oliver, reaching out and ringing the small bell sitting beside his coffee cup and saucer.

Within seconds Selina entered the room. She was wearing the uniform that Georgina had made for her while Oliver was away. It was grey, and styled after the fashion of Victorian Viennese parlour maids. It had a round neck with buttons down to the waist, and the bodice fitted closely. From there it draped softly down to her ankles, but Georgina had added a modern touch by leaving a split on the right side which reached a couple of inches above Selina's knee. As she walked across the room the split of the skirt opened to reveal that underneath she was wearing grey silk stockings, and high-heeled black shoes with a strap around the ankle that fastened with a tiny gold button.

Oliver knew, because Georgina had told him, that the material was coarse cotton, and since Selina had been forbidden to wear a bra, he could imagine how it must feel against her tender breasts so cruelly abused during the previous evening. As she removed his breakfast dishes he slid a hand up her leg until his fingers encountered the edge of her high-legged panties. He idly ran his hand over her hip for a few moments, his fingers splayed out so that they were able to feel the soft flesh of her lower belly, and Selina stood motionless, but for the faintest quiver which he could feel running through her. Eventually he removed his hand and glanced up at her.

'Carry on and clear the table please,' he said casually, and as she bent forward he grasped one of her breasts and squeezed hard. Selina gave a tiny moan of distress, and immediately Oliver removed the offending hand. 'I would prefer it if you remain silent when waiting on me,' he said casually. 'Perhaps this would be a good moment to tell you that if you ever disappoint me in your standard of service, I shall feel it my duty to punish you. Do you understand? And you may answer,' he added as she hesitated, clearly uncertain as to whether or not this was a trick.

'Yes, I suppose so,' she whispered, her eyes dazed.

After Selina had left the room, Georgina smiled at Oliver. 'I think you're right,' she said. 'Her body's very finely tuned already.'

'You have to remember that she's a total novice,' remarked Oliver. 'It's possible that she'll become less sensitive once she becomes accustomed to my particular brand of pleasure. But on the whole, I'm very pleased.'

Later that morning Oliver and Georgina strolled through the grounds of Summerfield Hall. Georgina, who didn't much care for excessive exercise, had no intention of traipsing around the whole acreage, so Oliver agreed that they settle for the herb garden, and while they were there Georgina suddenly put a hand to her mouth in shock. 'I forgot Kim!' she blurted.

'What do you mean, you forgot her?' asked Oliver, somewhat bemused. 'Where is she?'

'She's still tied to the bed,' explained Georgina. 'I'd better go and set her free. Poor little thing, she'll be in a terrible state by now.'

'Why don't you take Selina with you?' suggested Oliver, slyly.

'Is that wise?' asked Georgina. 'Remember, Kim's much further on in her training. And anyway, you and I don't have exactly the same tastes.'

'It will be interesting to see how she reacts,' said Oliver. 'Let's go and find her.'

Selina was in the kitchen, and she apprehensively watched them enter.

'Just a couple of things, Selina,' Oliver said. 'In the first place, I'm afraid I'm going to have to ask you to dismiss all the local staff. I'm having my own people brought up from London. It's far less troublesome for me to be surrounded by people who know the way I like things done.'

'You mean, I have to fire them all?' asked a horrified Selina.

'Do you have a problem with that?' he asked. 'They'll understand it's not your fault. You have told them that I'm the new owner, I hope?'

'Yes, of course,' she said hastily.

'Then blame me,' he said airily. 'And for the second thing, Georgina and I would like you to come with us for a moment. There's something you ought to see.'

Selina immediately put down the dish she'd been holding and followed the pair out of the kitchen, up the wide staircase, and along the landing to Georgina's bedroom. As the woman opened the door Oliver swiftly moved behind Selina, and guided her into the room. They closed the door and watched closely for her reaction to what she saw.

Kim was lying, spreadeagled and blindfolded, on the bed. She was entirely naked and her wrists had been handcuffed to the headboard. A bolster had been placed beneath her slim, almost boyish hips, and her legs were spread wide apart, kept in position by a wooden spreader-board that was firmly fastened around her ankles. She looked like an arched bow, with her belly thrust upwards and her arms and legs stretched so tightly that it was clearly hideously uncomfortable for her.

Oliver watched as Selina gave a tiny gasp and then swiftly turned towards the door. 'You stay,' he commanded. 'I want you to see this.'

'But—'

'There is no but,' snapped Oliver. 'Just watch, and remember.'

Georgina was already sitting on the edge of the bed, running one hand down the lean body, and the Oriental girl sighed at the touch.

'I'm so sorry,' cooed Georgina, her fingertips dancing lightly over the taut flesh as Kim uttered tiny cries of fear. 'How could I have forgotten you?'

'I don't understand,' whispered Selina, her eyes like saucers.

'Then watch,' said Oliver. 'You still have a lot to learn, my dear.'

Georgina's hands were now straying between Kim's stretched thighs, and lightly caressing the hairless pubic mound. With precise movements she opened the girl's sex, and then bending lower, began to lick gently around the soft inner tissue while Kim moaned pathetically and tried to pull her hips away from the tantalising tongue.

'Kim isn't allowed a climax today,' explained Georgina, her chin glistening with her victim's juices as she glanced

45

up at the bewitched Selina. 'She gave herself an extra orgasm last night without my permission, and so she knows that she has to go all day today without one. Isn't that right, my little treasure?' And she returned her tongue to the tormented girl.

Kim was making incoherent throaty sounds, and the tendons in her neck stood out tightly. It was clear that she was frantically trying to subdue her rising excitement, and then Georgina placed a palm on Kim's slim belly and began to massage it in firm circular motions. At the same time one finger located her clitoris. She gurgled and gasped from the pleasure as she visibly struggled to subdue the mounting threat of a blissful release.

'Remember what I said, my little treasure: no orgasms today,' Georgina reminded her poor captive.

Oliver smiled to himself; any fool could see that the girl was going to come. Georgina's finger was squelching in her copious juices, and her breathing was ragged. Every now and then it would snag in her throat, but he had to admire the way she was trying to subdue her over-excited flesh.

Suddenly he wanted Selina to join in. He wanted her to force the slim-hipped toy of Georgina's to fail in her denial, and then she would see for herself what was meant by punishment. 'Caress her breasts, my dear,' he whispered.

Selina looked at him aghast. 'No... I couldn't. Please don't ask that of me. I just can't do it... I can't.'

'Of course you can,' he urged. 'Besides, think of the pleasure you'll be giving her.'

'But she doesn't want pleasure,' she countered, confused. 'Didn't you hear what Georgina said?'

'Of course I heard!' he snapped. 'Don't you *ever* question me!'

Selina bowed her head. 'I'm sorry,' she apologised

meekly.

'Now I do hope you're not going to be silly about this, Selina,' he went on. 'Please don't disappoint me now.'

Selina knew she had little choice but to obey… or be thrown out of the house altogether. Very, very slowly she approached the blindfolded figure, and sat beside her, opposite Georgina. She tentatively reached out and cupped one soft breast.

'Go on,' Oliver urged.

'I don't know what to do,' she whispered innocently.

'Just stroke her very lightly,' directed Georgina. 'That's what she likes best… isn't it Kim?'

Finally the Oriental spoke. 'Please don't do as she asks,' she begged helplessly. 'I won't be able to stand it.'

'Go on,' Oliver urged again. 'I shan't tell you a third time, and if you're not careful it'll be you lying there instead of her.'

The threat spurred Selina into action. She lightly stroked the fleshy mounds. Kim writhed and twisted in her torment as Georgina continued to work busily between her thighs and her pink nipples began to harden under Selina's inexperienced touch.

'She's resisting very well,' remarked Oliver, with satisfaction.

'That's because she doesn't want to fail, isn't it Kimmie darling?' teased Georgina. 'But she will fail, because she just hasn't learnt enough self-control yet.'

Oliver could see the muscles of Kim's belly rippling as she struggled to stop the final contractions that would let her orgasm sweep over her. 'Lick her nipples, Selina,' he instructed, and watched as the girl obediently bent and gingerly touched the erect peaks with the tip of her tongue.

It all proved too much for the bound girl. With a scream of anguish she suddenly arched high off the bed as her climax tore through her, a climax so intense that when it was over she collapsed, pitifully sobbing and beseeching Georgina to deliver her from such torment.

Selina backed away from the bed and hovered indecisively, trembling from head to toe, but whether from fear or desire even she had no way of knowing.

Like a hungry wolf Oliver moved in. He wrapped his arms tightly around her. Her breasts crushed against him, and he felt her nipples hard inside the rough cotton fabric. Swiftly he unfastened the two top buttons of her bodice and slipped his fingers inside and over the throbbing buds. He tugged and squeezed until Selina's breathing began to quicken, and then he knew that despite her apparent horror, she was acutely excited by what she'd just seen and done.

Satisfied, he released her and opened the door. 'You can go now,' he said curtly to the dazed and somewhat bemused and disappointed girl. 'And fasten your dress. You look like a whore.'

After she'd hurried away in a flurry of skirts, Georgina looked at him. 'Well?' she asked. 'Did it go as you'd hoped?'

'Definitely,' he said with pleasure. 'I'll leave you to deal with your little plaything. No doubt you'll devise an interesting punishment for her, but I'd like to see her downstairs before lunch. She and Selina can both serve us. I think that would be a good idea, don't you?'

'Delightful,' agreed Georgina, and she and Oliver smiled knowingly at each other. As Georgina started to unfasten Kim's bonds Oliver left them alone. He would be interested to see what happened to Kim for the rest of the day, but he was far more interested in preparing an interesting evening for Selina. It would be an evening during which she would learn new things; not only how to receive, but also how to give.

As Selina loaded the dishwasher after dinner that evening, she wondered what on earth her father would think if he knew what was happening to her. The truth was that she didn't know what to think herself. Oliver Richards had come into her life like a terrifying prince of darkness, claiming her home and even her body. But she knew that somewhere, in some dark secret part of her soul she would never before have believed existed, she was pleased. Even witnessing and participating in the torment of Kim had aroused her beyond belief, despite the dreadful certainty that one day it would be her tied to the bed.

She felt ashamed, and yet excited. She supposed that she must be like her mother, just as her father had feared, which meant that even at the moment of the most intense pleasure the night before, she had been consumed by guilt. She knew that what she was doing was wrong, and even though she justified it by telling herself that she had no choice, she knew that wasn't strictly true. She was young and healthy. If she left the house she could make her own way in the world, but now, even after such a short time, she didn't want to leave because her body was revelling in its sudden freedom, a freedom that was undoubtedly dangerous, as well as liberating.

'I brought these dirty glasses,' said Kim, quietly slipping into the kitchen and interrupting Selina's confused thoughts. She held a couple of brandy balloons. 'They were in the study.'

'Thanks, I'm glad you found them,' said a relieved Selina. 'I imagine Oliver would have been very angry if they'd been left there.'

Kim nodded, and Selina took them from her.

'Would you tell me something?' she asked carefully.

Kim looked uncomfortable. 'Well, that depends on what you want to know,' she replied defensively.

'This morning – you know – when you were tied to the bed and...' Selina hesitated, the delicateness of the subject making her feel awkward, but Kim merely nodded her consent for her to proceed. '...Did you enjoy it?'

'Yes, of course I did,' Kim said quietly.

'How long had you been tied up like that?'

'Since the early hours of the morning.'

'But you must have been in pain,' Selina probed. 'Let me see your wrists.'

Kim held out her slim arms, and Selina saw that at each wrist the skin looked raw. 'Let me get something for that,' she said quickly.

Kim shook her head. 'You don't understand. I enjoy the pain.'

Selina understood – she understood only too well. Even now the memory of that exquisite pain that Oliver had caused to sear through her breasts the night before had the power to rekindle her desire. 'Were...' she stuttered, the recollection making her feel a little light-headed, 'were you punished for what happened... for having an orgasm?'

'Why do you want to know?' asked Kim. 'You'll never belong to Georgina. You're lucky – you're Oliver's.'

'But I need to know what the punishments are like,' said Selina. 'At the moment I keep imagining terrible things, and—'

'You're quite right to imagine terrible things,' the Oriental cut in. 'Especially as you belong to Oliver.'

'But I don't *belong* to him,' Selina said with firm conviction. 'I'm here because I *choose* to be.'

Kim smiled a little patronisingly. 'Of course you are...' she said – and said no more.

Selina felt somewhat belittled by the way the Oriental had virtually scorned her. 'You... you said I was lucky,' she said quietly. 'Lucky to be with Oliver. Have you ever been with him?'

Kim shook her head. 'Never. And I never will.'

'Why?'

'Because my first teacher was Christian Wells. He's Oliver's main rival at the Bar, and Oliver would never take someone that Christian had discarded. They're very competitive about everything, whether it's work or play.'

'What's Christian Wells like?' asked Selina.

'If you stay with Oliver you'll meet him,' said Kim. 'Even though they're arch rivals they always go to each other's dinner parties. You might even—' she stopped abruptly.

'Might even what?'

'It doesn't matter,' said Kim, and then she moved away, showing obvious agitation, just as Georgina gracefully swept into the kitchen.

'And what are you two gossiping about?' demanded the elegant woman.

'Nothing… Kim just brought some glasses in for me to wash,' Selina said hastily.

'Kim can do those,' Georgina said to her. 'You must go up to your room and get changed. Oliver wants to talk to you this evening. I've put out the clothes he wants you to wear. They're on your bed.'

Selina's stomach lurched as excitement and fear mingled, and she trembled with anticipation for what might lay ahead.

Georgina looked at her thoughtfully. 'You're becoming addicted already, aren't you?' she said slowly. 'You'd better be careful Selina, this is merely the tip of the iceberg. Oliver brings a new meaning to the word *depravity*.'

Selina sensed that the woman was not exaggerating. But she also sensed that Oliver wouldn't want to hear such talk, and she wondered why Georgina was trying to make her more anxious than she already was.

Once in her room she hurried to the bed and stared at what lay on the duvet. It looked like an old-fashioned corset.

Guessing that time was short, she hastily peeled off her grey housekeeper's dress, washed, and then stepped into the black figure-hugging body-shaper. It had a basque-style top with black lacing, while the high cut-away legs were edged with matching lace, and there was a zip at the crotch. Also on the bed were a pair of silk hold-up stockings, high-heeled shoes, and a pair of elbow-length gloves, all in black.

When she was dressed she studied her appearance in the mirror on her wardrobe door. She could hardly believe what she saw. With her dark chestnut curls tumbling around her shoulders and her soft hazel eyes wide with both excitement and trepidation, her full breasts spilling out of the cups and her tiny waist and taut buttocks all accentuated by the garment, she looked both wanton and yet innocent at the same time.

Feeling extremely uncertain about everything, she made her way down to the dining room where Oliver had initiated her so devastatingly only twenty-four hours before.

She tapped gingerly on the heavy wooden door.

'Come in!' called Oliver.

He was dressed casually in dark green slacks and a short-sleeved beige cotton shirt, open at the neck. He smiled at Selina, and she smiled nervously back at him.

'You look delightful,' he said approvingly. 'Not at all like the girl I met here late last Sunday night.'

'I am the same girl,' said Selina softly.

Oliver laughed, and she shivered, because the laughter seemed to mock her. 'Hardly,' he murmured. 'Don't tell me you've forgotten last night?' Selina shook her head. 'I thought not. In fact, it would have been a severe blow to my ego if you had.

'Walk over to the window,' he said abruptly, his mood

changing.

Without hesitating, Selina turned and moved towards the huge bay, and as she walked she was aware that because of the tightness of the body-shaper and the height of the stiletto heels, she was moving provocatively, her hips swaying, but there was nothing she could do about it. When she reached the window and turned to face Oliver she could tell that this had been the intention.

'Very nice indeed…' he said pensively. 'Is there anyone outside?'

Selina glanced over her shoulder. It was still light despite being nearly eight-thirty, and she realised the gardener was still working not too far away, tidying the edges of the vast lawn. 'Yes,' she told him. 'The gardener, Riley.'

'Excellent,' smiled Oliver. 'Then I think our evening can now begin.'

Chapter Four

Selina watched as Oliver advanced towards her. His expression was stern. There was no hint of affection or softness in his features, and yet she felt a surge of desire and her breasts ached with the need to again feel his mouth on them. He began to unfasten the silk ribbons at the front of the basque-like garment. When they were loosened the rigid material burst apart and her milk-white breasts sprung forth before his admiring gaze.

She breathed a tiny sigh of contentment, and he spitefully flicked her nipples, a stinging blow that made her jerk with shock.

'I prefer silence at this stage,' he snapped, and Selina wondered how she was supposed to suppress every tiny sound.

Without warning he gripped her shoulders and spun her to face the window. At that moment the gardener looked up. Poor Selina was horrified, and tried to shrink back and drew her arms up to cover her exposed breasts.

'Keep your arms down,' he ordered.

'But he can see me!' she protested.

Oliver smiled, but there was no amusement there. 'That's the whole idea. I want him to see what a wanton hussy you really are.'

'No, please, that's not fair!'

'Fair? I don't remember ever mentioning the word fair. You promised to obey me, remember? This is what I want you to do, and if I choose for you to have an audience then that's the way it will be. Believe me, if you learn as fast as

I suspect you will, then within a few weeks this will seem like nothing at all.'

Selina didn't think she could possibly obey him this time. She'd known old Riley for so long that the thought of him watching her now, seeing her naked breasts and watching as Oliver lazily fondled them, was unthinkable. Yet despite her shame, shards of excitement were making her skin prickle and she could feel a lovely ache between her thighs.

Slowly, her arms lowered. Oliver gripped her waist and with consummate ease he lifted her onto a high chair by the window. He moved around her, being careful not to block the gardener's view, and stooped a little to lick each nipple in turn, his tongue lazily caressing the stiffening buds. He was incredibly gentle, moving from nipple to nipple and occasionally lapping at the undersides of each breast, which he would lift and nuzzle with his nose and lips as though trying to drown himself in their succulent warmth. As he worshipped each glorious mound of flesh Selina's eyelids grew heavy with rising desire, and her head lolled back as she relaxed into the pleasure of it all.

Then, with shocking abruptness, Oliver's teeth bit savagely on her left nipple and despite his earlier instruction, Selina was unable to suppress a scream as dreadful pain shot through her breast. But even as her cry died away the pain turned into the strange dark pleasure that she was beginning to crave, and her tormented nerves sent signals of desire down through her belly and deeper still, until a tiny pulse began to drum behind her clitoris.

Selina's eyes flew open and she gazed into his sombre face in hurt puzzlement. She opened her mouth to question him, to ask why he had done such a thing, but then she remembered what he'd said earlier and said nothing, and Oliver nodded in silent approval. This outward expression of his satisfaction gave her incredible pleasure. She longed to wrap her arms round his neck and pull his head back to her breasts, but she knew she would never ever dare to act unbidden.

'Look out of the window,' said Oliver huskily, his hands moving between her thighs and slowly unfastening the zip that held the crotch closed. Selina did, and saw that Riley, his well-worn cap pushed to the back of his head, was watching in stunned disbelief, his eyes bulging and his face flushed. Selina hung her head in shame, but Oliver put his fingers beneath her chin and forced it up again so that she had no choice but to look into the gawking gardener's eyes. From the waist down he was blocked from view by an ornate hedge, but in the growing gloom she realised by the furtive movements of one arm that he was playing with himself! The sight of her being fondled by the new owner of Summerfield Hall was enough to make him need to masturbate, right in front of her eyes! Never in her life had she felt so degraded... yet a tiny sigh of delight escaped her slightly parted lips.

'It seems you have difficulty in controlling your vocalisation,' said Oliver, lifting her down from the chair and moving her to the centre of the room. 'That's a fault I shall have to correct immediately. It could spoil many an interesting moment, although there will be times when I shall want to hear every sound you wish to make.'

'I don't understand why you're doing all this to me,' said Selina despairingly. 'With every other liberty you're taking with me, what does it matter to you whether I make a noise or not?'

'It matters because I have to be in control,' said Oliver sternly. 'Whether I'm working or playing I like everything to be as I wish it, and tonight I wish for peace and quiet.' He paused for a moment. 'You'll understand better in time,' he added, his voice not unkind. 'If you stay the course, if you learn the way the game is played, then I can offer you pleasure such as you would never otherwise know it. Doesn't that thought excite you?'

It did, and his words conjured up strange dark images; images that scarcely made sense but which had the power to arouse her newly awakened flesh, and suddenly she was eager to discover what was going to happen next. She didn't have long to wait.

Oliver retied the laces on the basque and closed it back over her breasts. Then he sat down and, without a word of explanation, pulled her over his knees. Her head hung down so that her lustrous hair brushed the carpet, and he straightened her legs until she could only balance on her toes, her taut thigh muscles complaining.

With one swift movement he unfastened the zip that ran down the back of the garment, leaving her naked from shoulder to hip, and then she felt him fumble in his pocket for a moment. Something soft tickled her spine. It was as though he was trailing a cord up and down her back, and then lower to the cleft between her buttocks. He prised the garment further apart and fully exposed her creamy buttocks. Now she could feel the cord trailing over them, and squirmed against his lap because the feeling was both gentle and arousing. There was also a pleasant lump pressing up against her belly.

Selina was totally unprepared for the sudden sharp cracking sound that was swiftly followed by a scorching pain right across the cheeks of her bottom. It was a pain sharper than anything she'd experienced before, and she cried out.

'You really must learn to keep quiet,' admonished Oliver. 'This is your punishment for not controlling yourself properly by the window. Every time you cry out now the punishment will only go on longer.'

'Bu-but you're hurting me,' protested Selina, desperately trying to wriggle away from him.

He placed a large hand firmly in the small of her back, pinning her down against his thighs, and despite everything she automatically ground her hips so that her pubic mound was stimulated by the pressure.

He laughed confidently. 'Yes, it's just as I thought,' he said, and then she heard the dreadful cracking sound again and once more the pain seared through her, scolding the cheeks of her bottom. The hot sensation spread through to her belly, but as it did so it turned into a different kind of heat; a glowing warmth that began to infuse her abdomen and engorge her pelvic area as her excitement increased. She made no further sound, and even when she received four more lashes from the tiny riding crop she bravely remained silent, but all the time the shocking arousal mounted until she was writhing wantonly on his lap.

'That's better,' Oliver said calmly. 'It seems you can control yourself, when you want to.' He delved between her limp thighs and found her engorged clitoris. To her mortification the first faintest touch made her spasm in a moment of delicious pleasure as the pent-up longing and tension of all that had preceded it exploded in a moment of ecstasy.

Oliver barely waited for her to stop convulsing before he refastened the zip and rolled her off his lap so that she sprawled at his feet, gazing up at him in confusion.

'Now it's time you learnt to give *me* some pleasure,' he said firmly. 'Kneel up.' For a moment she didn't move, so he raised the crop and lashed it down viciously across her unprotected shoulders. It hurt, and she scrambled up onto her knees.

Her face was now level with his crotch, and without ceremony Oliver unzipped his slacks and freed his straining cock from his shorts. It sprang out at Selina, fully erect, the gnarled veins clearly visible. His glans was a deep purple and Selina stared in fascination, unable to believe the size and girth of it. It throbbed before her spellbound eyes, like a waking serpent preparing to strike. She couldn't imagine why she had to kneel there, but continued to stare in fascination at the first male erection she'd seen in her life, and once again she felt a hungry pulse beating between her thighs.

'I want you to make love to me with your mouth,' announced Oliver. 'I don't suppose you know what to do, do you?'

Selina's fingers entwined anxiously, and she looked up at him. 'No,' she whispered, hoping her response wouldn't cause the crop to rise and fall again.

'I will use your mouth just as I used your pussy last night,' he explained matter-of-factly. 'Part your lips,' he added, and only then did she begin to understand.

She withdrew instinctively, but he was too quick for her and grasped the back of her neck and pulled her towards him with one angry yank. 'Didn't you hear what I said?' he demanded, and despite her abhorrence Selina obeyed, because she was more concerned of the consequences if she didn't.

As soon as her moist lips peeled apart Oliver thrust his swollen member between them. 'Open wider,' he ordered sharply. 'And don't you dare nip me with your teeth!' Selina's jaw began to ache as she strained to obeyed. He was so long and thick that it was difficult for her. Her lips were stretched taut, and then the tip of his penis nudged the back of her throat and for a moment she feared she would gag.

'Good,' he suddenly said and withdrew. 'Now we'll start at the beginning.'

Utterly bewildered but grateful for the brief respite, Selina sank back onto her haunches.

'I want you to use your imagination,' he went on. 'I want you to lick, to suck, to be creative. Do anything you feel will excite me – but I don't want to feel your teeth.'

His requirements and warning were clear enough. Selina really didn't want to do anything for the man, but she was drawn by the awesome power of his erection, and by the animal scent of it. Knowing she had little choice she tentatively licked at the underside of the spearing shaft, and her courage grew. When she heard a sharp breath hiss into his lungs her confidence grew too. She slowly warmed to her task, sucking and licking, moving her fingers up and down the base of the shaft, and as she licked the smooth glans she saw a tiny drop of clear fluid ooze from the eye at the tip. Without stopping to consider what she was doing she licked it away with a tiny flick of her tongue, and immediately felt Oliver's body tense. His claw-like fingers dug into her shoulders and his hips eased forward.

The erotic tension in his body was incredibly arousing for Selina. After a few minutes she became totally engulfed in what she was doing, experimenting with speed and pressure, varying the rhythm of her fingers and her tongue, occasionally halting all activity, and only beginning again when she feared he might strike her. She could tell that by keeping him on edge, uncertain as to what he should expect, she was increasing his arousal as well as her own.

After long electric minutes he buried his hands in her luxurious hair and pulled her face away from where it was buried in the humid warmth of his groin, his cock throbbing against her forehead as she experimentally nuzzled his hanging balls. 'Open your mouth now,' he croaked, his voice thick with desire, and this time she was happy to obey, although as he slowly slid between her lips she again experienced the fear of choking. Once more she made a tiny movement of retreat, a movement he swiftly checked, and he then held her firmly in place as he started to thrust his hips back and forth with increasing ferocity. A slightly salty taste permeated her mouth. Oliver moved faster, regardless of the discomfort to Selina. His head rocked back and he went rigid. A groan seemed to be wrenched from the very depths of his being. Selina was terrified, fearing he was having a heart attack, and then he exploded into her mouth and she felt the glutinous fluid sliding down her throat.

She wanted to withdraw then, but his hands were like iron fists in her hair and she was forced remain still. 'Suck me,' he hissed. 'Milk it all from me,' and she had no choice but to obey, her mouth moving quickly.

At last she felt him begin to soften in her mouth, and then he relaxed and withdrew. He sank onto a chair, his head lolling back and his legs sprawled out, his rapidly diminishing erection laying sticky and harmless against his thigh.

Selina didn't know what to do, so she started to get to her feet, but immediately Oliver's half closed eyes opened a little wider. 'Did I give you permission to move?' he said.

'No,' she answered miserably.

'You disappoint me, Selina,' he said quietly. 'It's a shame when you've done fairly well so far, but you must remember that whenever you're in my presence you are under my command.'

Fairly well? Selina felt humiliated and demoralised, but she didn't respond because she knew that too would be an infringement of the rules. She remained kneeling meekly before the slowly recovering man, the potent taste of him on her lips and tongue.

After a few minutes Oliver stood up and casually rearranged his clothing. 'You may stand up now,' he said curtly, and she climbed unsteadily to her feet, accidentally knocking against him as she did so. He made no comment, but she could see from the expression in his eyes that she'd compounded her previous error.

'Now I have to decide how to punish you,' he said. 'And it's such a shame, because I was going to give you a little reward for your valiant efforts to please me.' He thought for a moment, and then glanced out of the window where dusk was just beginning to fall. 'I know,' he said suddenly. 'We'll take a stroll in the grounds.'

'Has Riley gone?' Selina asked anxiously.

Oliver looked at her in amazement. 'Is it really so very difficult to keep quiet and simply obey?' he asked. Selina didn't say anything, and meekly allowed him to guide her out of the room and towards the gardens.

Once outside Selina shivered. Her glowing flesh was abruptly chilled by the cool night air, which also stiffened her aching nipples. 'I want you to collect some birch twigs,' said Oliver, pointing in the direction of a nearby tree. Without questioning him Selina walked across the lawn, hoping against hope that no one could see her as she bent down and exposed her tender bottom and the crotch pressed against her swollen sex lips.

When she had a good collection of twigs she returned to Oliver, slightly bemused as to why he needed them.

Oliver glanced briefly at them and nodded. 'That should be enough, bring them back inside.'

Once back in the dining room Selina stood silently, watching in puzzlement as Oliver tied the twigs together, and then he looked at her thoughtfully. 'Undress,' he said.

'Completely?' asked Selina.

'Completely,' he confirmed. 'I want you naked for this.'

Still unaware of what lay ahead for her, Selina removed her skimpy clothing and gave a tiny sigh of relief as the tight restrictions of the body-shaper were removed.

'Now lie face down on the table,' instructed Oliver, and Selina quickly pressed her body against the cool mahogany surface, taking an inexplicable pleasure in pressing herself against the unyielding wood and surreptitious agitating her nipples against it. She heard Oliver snigger, and then he manoeuvred her so that she was spread full length and only her feet hung over the polished edge.

'Grip the sides of the table,' he said, and again she obeyed.

Long silent minutes passed. Selina tensed, and her anxiety returned. She held her breath. What was he doing? She tried to peer over her shoulder to see.

'Head down,' he snapped.

Something was trailed up the backs of her legs, and up over her rounded buttocks, still sore from where the crop had struck her.

She realised it must be the bunch of birch twigs, and at exactly that moment she realised too what was going to happen next.

The whippy twigs bit spitefully. Selina forced back the cry that began deep in her lungs, and gripped the table even harder until her knuckles glowed white.

Oliver didn't strike her too hard, but he moved methodically over the entire length of her body. It wasn't a pain at all, but a delicious pleasure, a stimulation that made her belly ache even more, and she could feel the moisture seeping from between her thighs – a shaming condemnation.

When every inch of her back, buttocks, and legs were glowing Oliver gripped her waist and turned her over like a rag doll. She was forced to lie there, looking up at him as he held the bundle of twigs and contemplated her.

'Where shall I begin?' he mused, gently touching her breasts, before moving lower across her softly rounded belly. Then he spread her legs and continued his investigation between her thighs. She stiffened in horror. 'Keep still,' he ordered. She didn't dare protest. 'Bend your knees and place the soles of your feet on the table.'

Selina knew now what was going to happen, but there was nothing she could do to prevent it. She wanted to be touched differently, to be caressed and stroked, only she had no choice because she was the servant and he was the master.

Oliver coldly watched the conflicting expressions flit across her face, and as she stared up at him she felt the tears spring from her eyes.

'It will be good in the end,' he promised, his voice caressing, and then he pushed her knees wide apart.

Selina closed her eyes and waited.

The twigs swished through the still air and bit into her vulnerable thighs. Oliver was clearly a master at his trade, working his way down the length of her inner thighs, and moving from her right to left with scarcely a pause until her body heaved and contracted as the waves of dark pleasure and pain began to wash upwards, engulfing her.

Finally he struck lightly across her flat stomach, until that too was a delicate shade of pink, and only then did he discard the instrument of her torment. Without offering her respite he thrust three fingers deep inside her while at the same time his thumb stroked her clitoris, and she could feel the traitorous bud hardening under the knowing caresses.

She was on the point of coming. Her head rolled from side to side and her breasts rose and swelled as she gasped to fill her lungs. Her sore back arched and lifted off the polished surface. She was coming… and then the bastard abruptly withdrew his fingers and left her totally bereft, teetering on the edge of a climax that had been slowly building for so long.

'And that is your punishment,' he said coldly. 'Now get dressed and get out.'

Selina couldn't believe that even Oliver could be so horribly cruel, but he merely stared implacably at her as she began to cry. She sat on the table, her nipples protruding stiffly from the dark areolae, making her arousal all the more evident. She looked at him in mute appeal, but he turned away, as though tired of her.

'Why are you doing this to me?' she cried. 'Why do you keep punishing me for every little thing I do wrong? I'm trying my hardest, can't you see that?'

'Trying isn't good enough,' retorted Oliver. 'I demand perfection in everyone and everything. I thought you understood that.'

'But not straight away!' Selina protested.

'If I tell anyone something once I don't expect to have to repeat myself,' he explained curtly. 'You're a quick learner, Selina, but I think you lack concentration. You seem to get lost in the pleasures of the flesh all too easily. As yet you're failing to combine discipline with your newfound sexuality. It should all come to you... in time.'

'I don't think I can bear much more if this is how it's going to be,' she cried. 'You don't understand how I feel,' and as she spoke she started to massage her aching breasts.

'Stop that!' snarled Oliver. 'If you can't bear it, leave. No one's forcing you to stay here, and your complaining is becoming rather tiresome. No get out of my sight before I really lose my temper!'

Once more Selina found herself in the humiliating position of having to collect her discarded clothing and leave the room feeling embarrassed by her own lascivious wanting. Yet even as she passed by Oliver she felt a powerful surge of sexual attraction towards him, and knew that no matter what happened she wouldn't be leaving Summerfield Hall.

Once in her bedroom she threw herself face down on the bed and cried bitter tears of frustration. Her whole body was pulsating with desire and her lower belly and breasts ached desperately due to her lack of orgasm. Without quite realising what she was doing she squeezed a hand between her belly and the duvet. Her fingers inched through her soft pubic hair until at last they brushed against the still erect clitoris that hid there. They immediately began to move faster. Within seconds she could feel the first tiny convulsions beginning to grip her body, and then there was an inner explosion and wave after wave of sheer bliss overwhelmed her.

'Well, well...' said a horribly familiar voice from the door. 'And what have we here then?'

It was far too late for Selina to do anything. She continued to lie face down until her climax finally ebbed away, and then she turned over and curled into a protective ball as she looked across the bedroom at the watchful Oliver.

'Didn't you hear what I said to you downstairs?' he asked, his anger evident beneath his outer calm.

'Yes... well, that is...'

'Of course you did,' he said irritably. He frowned and then nodded. 'I can understand now why your father kept you away from the outside world. Clearly you're just as lascivious as your mother was. Just as disobedient too, it would appear. How long is it going to take you to learn the basic lessons, Selina? Not until you've mastered them can we move on to the more interesting aspects of our relationship. I'm anxious to take you to London to show you off to my friends there, but you're nowhere near ready yet. You're going to have to learn once and for all that I simply won't tolerate any kind of disobedience.'

'What are you going to do to me?' she whimpered.

'You'll see soon enough.'

His tone filled Selina with dread, and she cringed back as he strode determinedly across the room, snatched her wrists, and pulled her sobbing and protesting out of the room and along the landing to his. Once inside he quickly found a silk scarf in one of his drawers, tied her hands securely behind her back, and then knotted the loose end to the post at the foot of the bed.

'Please, please don't do this to me,' she begged, but he contemptuously ignored her pleading.

'I'm going to bed now,' he said. 'I'm extremely tired, and I don't expect to be disturbed by you. You'd better prey I get a good night's sleep, because if I don't I'll hold you responsible, and then you'll discover the delights of the dungeon rather earlier than I'd intended.'

Selina said nothing more. The very thought of the converted cellar was almost enough to make her legs crumple beneath her. And now, with her newfound knowledge, she could imagine only too well some of the contraptions that might have gone down into that macabre room.

Oliver disappeared into the *en suite*. For a few minutes she could hear his ablutions, and then he reappeared wearing a luxurious bathrobe. He slipped it off, and climbed smoothly between the silk sheets.

'Not a sound, now,' he warned finally, and then extinguished the bedside lamp.

Selina stood in the enveloping darkness. She was naked, cold, and tied to the bedpost. She knew she wouldn't be able to sleep. Within a few minutes it was clear from the sound of Oliver's slow breathing that he had already dropped off, and Selina knew it was going to be a long, long night.

Oliver woke early, and through the early morning light filtering through the heavy curtains he saw the lovely contours of Selina standing motionless at the end of the bed.

Propping himself on one elbow he could see she was drifting in and out of a tormented doze. He jumped out of bed and drew back the curtains so he could have a good look at her. With her arms pinned back her wonderful breasts were jutting forward in all their glory.

Her eyes were gaunt through lack of sleep, her lips slightly parted in mute appeal as she stared at him, clearly longing for some word of comfort or praise. From the streaks on her cheeks he guessed that at some point during the night she had cried. But the tears had long since dried, and if anything there was now an air of slight defiance about her which both impressed him and increased his desire to force her into total submission.

'Good morning, Selina,' he said briskly. She didn't answer him. 'You can speak freely this morning,' he assured her. 'It's a new day. I'm in a better mood and your noise won't bother me.'

He moved close and stooped slightly to run a hand up between her thighs, letting the tips of his fingers caress the sensitive skin and causing her legs to tremble. Selina groaned softly. He probed between her slick sex lips. Her knees buckled, and she would have fallen but for the restraining scarf.

'It seems your night of bondage and denial gave you some pleasure,' he remarked dryly.

Selina nodded, but she seemed unable to speak, completely overwhelmed by the long night, and he pondered the cocktail of emotions she must have experienced while he slept.

'You look tired,' he added.

'I am,' she whispered.

He began to touch her between her thighs again, and when he reached the swollen nub of pleasure already proudly erect she inhaled sharply.

'And not only tired, it seems,' he murmured. This time she didn't answer, but her body spoke for her, and he continued with his skilful manipulation of the damp tissue surrounding her clitoris, occasionally allowing one finger to slide inside her, teasing the entrance to her vagina. She started to thrust towards him, and her hips moved restlessly while tiny whimpering sounds of need issued from her mouth as he worked.

Oliver's erection was huge. Selina's eyes were fixed on the bulbous helmet, and the tip of her tongue moistened her lips. He knew he had to have her there and then, no matter how she felt or what she really wanted.

He pressed himself against her, pinning her back against the bedpost. For a moment he caressed her silky hair as he savoured the feel of her soft breasts against his ribs and her flat stomach sandwiching his cock against his lower belly. Then he clutched the post above her head for support as he cupped and lifted her buttocks with his free hand.

'Wrap your legs around my waist,' he grunted through clenched teeth, and as she obeyed he eased into her with one long slow penetration. Selina's mouth opened in a silent scream, and once he was filling her completely he paused and relished the exquisite tightness of her cunt.

'Shit, you feel good!' he snorted, and then began rutting against her, the bed creaking as he shunted her rhythmically back against the post.

'Ah – am I allowed to come now?' she begged frantically,

just before his mouth covered hers in a kiss that was unexpectedly tender.

'Yes,' he panted when he broke away, and they ground against each other, totally consumed by their mutual need for release. As Oliver erupted Selina stiffened and her head flopped back, rolling helplessly from side to side, and her perspiring body shuddered beneath his onslaught.

As soon as his powerful orgasm had subsided Oliver disentangled himself from her clutching limbs, and stepped back to admire the girl in all her post-coital beauty.

'If you could only see yourself now,' he said quietly, and then an idea struck him. Releasing her wrists he carried her across the room so that she was forced to gaze at herself in his full length mirror, and he saw the shock cross her innocent face as her eyes took in the evidence of their recent lust-filled coupling.

'I promised you delights beyond your imagination, didn't I?' he reminded her. 'This is nothing. I can take you to places you never dreamed existed, Selina, as long as you trust me.'

'I don't think I'm brave enough,' she said sadly.

'Of course you are,' he said, and then he carried her back and lay her on the bed. 'Get some sleep now. You'll need all your strength over the next few days. I have something rather special planned for you. It's time we moved forward another step. The days are passing and we have to proceed quickly. There's still so much for you to learn.'

He wasn't certain whether Selina heard his last words or not, because by the time he'd finished speaking her eyes were closed, her mind and body totally exhausted by all that she'd endured.

Chapter Five

By two o'clock that afternoon Selina had enjoyed a long soak in a hot bath, and changed into her grey housekeeper's uniform so she could get the house organised for the evening meal. She still hadn't plucked up enough courage to tell the staff that they were surplus to requirements, and as a result she felt extremely uncomfortable in their presence.

Oliver didn't invite her to join him and Georgina for dinner, and there was no sign of Kim anywhere, which made Selina feel rather apprehensive.

At nine o'clock Georgina and Oliver were still in the dining room drinking and chatting, and Selina went in to see if there was anything more they wanted. Oliver looked at her and smiled. Selina's spirits sank. She'd already learned that when he smiled like that it usually meant trouble.

'Ah Selina, we were just talking about you,' he said. 'It's time for you to change now.'

'You're providing the evening's entertainment,' added Georgina, and she smiled too.

'But I – I only came in to see if you needed anything more,' she said hastily.

'We do... we need you,' said Oliver. He rose quickly and slipped an arm around her waist. 'It's time for a little indulgence in the playroom.'

'Selina hasn't seen it since I had it redecorated,' said Georgina.

'That's true,' agreed Oliver. 'Well, we'd better correct that little oversight right now.'

Without another word the couple guided her out of the dining room, through the front door, and along the path towards the bridge that crossed into the old wing of the house. She felt her heart thumping against her ribs, and suddenly she just had to get away from them. She twisted from his hold and turned to flee back to the main house. Taken by surprise Oliver let her go, but she'd only run a few yards when he caught up with her, snatching an arm around her waist again and scooping her up against him.

'What the hell do you think you're playing at?' He was obviously angry. 'Do you want to leave, is that it?'

'I don't know what I want any more,' cried Selina, disturbed by his dangerous mood swings. 'But I'm afraid.'

'Fear is an excellent aphrodisiac,' said Oliver, with a wolfish glint in his eye. 'A fact that you've already discovered. Come along. And I don't want any more of this infantile stupidity.'

'But...'

'Oh let her go,' said Georgina contemptuously. 'Kim is already waiting for us. It looks as though you were wrong about this girl.' She indicated Selina dismissively.

Selina looked at Georgina, and saw a tiny sparkle of scornful triumph in her blue eyes. It somehow rekindled her courage. 'I won't run away again,' she promised, and Oliver nodded, but gripped her very tightly as he hustled her over the bridge and into the foreboding wing of the house.

The playroom was a revelation to Selina. It had been repainted in cream and green, and carpeted. There was a strange white table with thick leather straps attached to it, a number of chrome and white chairs, and even what looked like a folding bed. Clinically white cupboards and work surfaces lined two of the walls. In one corner there was a large basin, and above that was what looked like a medicine cupboard. Certainly it wasn't like any playroom that Selina had ever seen before. It was more like a doctor's surgery, and Oliver had the air of a medical man and Georgina his assistant.

'And where's Kim?' asked Oliver.

'Down in the dungeon,' Georgina told him. 'I'll go and get her.'

As the voluptuous woman opened the door to what had previously been the cellar, Selina saw that the rickety old steps had been replaced by a modern steel flight, and the light could now be switched on from the playroom, making it far easier and safer to descend.

Georgina disappeared, and Selina looked anxiously at Oliver. 'Am I allowed to make any noise this evening?' she asked hesitantly, and feeling a little self-conscious for having to ask such a question.

'You can make as much noise as you like at any time,' said Oliver. 'There are no rules tonight. All you have to do is accept this new discipline without question.'

'What new discipline?' she asked, none too happy with what she was hearing.

'It's simply another stage in your learning process.'

But before she could ask him more she heard soft sobbing as Kim was led up the metal steps and into the room. At the sight of her Selina gasped in dismay.

Kim was totally naked, except for a black leather collar to which a leash was attached, a leash held by Georgina, who was pulling the unresisting girl further into the room. There were red weals criss-crossing the Oriental girl's breasts and belly, and she looked as though she hadn't slept for ages. She looked at Selina with dull eyes, and yet when Georgina suddenly tugged her close and kissed her enflamed breasts Kim's pink nipples instantly puckered, and Selina could see she was acutely aroused.

'Don't worry,' said Oliver. 'I'm not planning to do that to you. This is going to be a very special night, Selina. Kim is helping because what we're going to teach you is something that she adores. Isn't that true, Kim?'

The lovely Oriental nodded submissively, her hair falling like jet-black curtains in front of her face as she did so.

'Say yes,' prompted Georgina, emphasising her authority by tugging on the leash.

'Yes, Mr Richards,' Kim whispered. 'I like it very much.'

'There you are,' said Oliver with satisfaction. 'Now then Selina, your evening begins.'

The poor girl watched as Georgina led Kim to the table and bent her forward across its surface. One hand between Kim's shoulders was enough for the dominant woman to keep her slave obediently in position. Selina could see there were also raised weals striping the unfortunate girl's taut buttocks and upper thighs.

'You look a little overdressed, Selina,' Oliver commented. 'Take your clothes off.'

She obediently slipped off the grey dress, grateful that she'd not worn any underwear, as instructed.

'Leave the stockings on,' he continued. 'I do love a gorgeous girl in stockings.'

Georgina studied Selina and smiled, clearly in salacious agreement with her partner.

'Now,' Selina's attention was brought back to Oliver, 'I want you to watch what I'm going to do very carefully,' he explained. 'It's all easy enough for Kim, she's used to it, but when I've finished with her it'll be your turn. It will prove more difficult for you, but not so much more that I expect you to fail.'

Selina frowned, still not understanding him fully, but certain that whatever his intention it would involve more humiliation and pain; hopefully of the kind for which she was beginning to yearn.

From one of the drawers Georgina took a long white cylindrical implement. It was wide of girth at the base and tapered down towards the tip.

Selina had seen nothing like it before, but Oliver held it up and gazed upon it reverently as though it was something of religious consequence. When ready he turned to the girl prepared for him on the table, and carefully parted the cheeks of her bottom, revealing the tiny puckered opening that nestled there. Georgina took the lid off a small tube of gel and passed it to him, whereupon he massaged some of it into the deep valley, causing his victim to squirm slightly. Selina noticed that her straining legs had tightened in anticipation of what was to come.

When satisfied with his preparations, Oliver eased the tip of the strange implement against the tiny opening, and then with a slow rotating movement, he eased it inside the bent girl.

Selina stood openmouthed, barely able to believe what she was seeing. Surely nobody did things like that!

'Ooohhh… it's so *thick*,' the skewered girl protested.

'Nonsense,' chided Oliver, reminding Selina more and more of a doctor.

'She may be a little sore from last night,' chuckled Georgina.

Showing no regard for Kim, Oliver continued to press, and the girl sighed as her tight ring of muscle stretched to allow the thickening object inside. She groaned again, and would have arched off the table if it hadn't been for the firm hand on her back.

'Oh for goodness sake behave,' admonished her mistress. 'You know you can accommodate more than that.'

'But it *is* too big,' protested Kim, straining to look up over her shoulder at her two tormentors. Her dark eyes were wide and sparkling, but whether from wicked pleasure or genuine fear, Selina couldn't tell.

'Ignore her,' said Georgina dismissively. 'The naughty little darling is in one of her moods.' With that she curled her fingers in Kim's glossy black hair and tugged her head up. Kim yelped as her neck muscles were contorted into a direction they didn't want to go, but her protest was smothered as Georgina swooped and kissed her deeply. Oliver's activity intensified. He mauled the girl's tight buttocks with one hand and his elbow sawed as he began to pump the invasive white plastic back and forth, and as Selina watched the girl trapped on the table suddenly shuddered and whimpered into her mistress's mouth as she enjoyed a tiny orgasm.

Selina was stunned. In her wildest secret thoughts she had never imagined anything of the like, and she couldn't imagine that she, or anybody else for that matter, would ever receive pleasure from it.

Suddenly she longed to flee from these monstrous people... but where to?

And, if she was truly honest with herself, could she really exist now without the dark desires she was beginning to hunger for?

Utterly bewildered, she remained rooted to the spot, unable to tear her eyes from the outrageous vision of Oliver slowly withdrawing the wicked tool from Kim's bottom.

'There, you see.' Selina realised Oliver had turned and was talking to her. 'I told you she enjoys it. Now it's your turn.'

Selina shook her head. 'Oh no... please don't do that to me,' she begged. 'I really don't want you to.'

'Now you know you do,' he coaxed. 'Hasn't there always been pleasure so far? You have to learn to trust as well as obey. Come along now, don't let me down in front of

Georgina.'

Georgina had allowed Kim to rise and she was now standing quietly, head bowed, in one corner.

'I don't want to,' repeated Selina, without real conviction, and Oliver simply pushed her towards the strange table, and she automatically bent forward. Georgina held her naked shoulders and guided her down until her breasts flattened against the stark surface. Selina shuddered, feeling as though she was being prepared for an operation.

There was an uncomfortable pause, and then Oliver broke the silence.

'You saw what I did to Kim,' he stated, rather than asked. Selina nodded. 'Now, this will just feel a little cold,' he added, and then he was parting the cheeks of her bottom and a finger insinuated its way between them and dabbed the cool gel around her virginal opening. Selina cringed at the feel of the rude invasion. He continued his task, and then popped a finger just inside her, easing the path for what was to come. Selina shifted anxiously under the alien touch.

Georgina chuckled. 'I think she'll enjoy this,' she remarked, to nobody in particular.

Selina gripped the edge of the table as she felt the tip of the greased implement probe at her anus. She tensed, instinctively trying to repel the invader, but Oliver raised his hand and administered a stinging slap to one bare buttock. Selina jerked and yelped with shock, horrified at the indignity of it all.

'Do not defy me,' he warned from over her shoulder.

'I – I'm sorry,' she sobbed, the tears beginning to squeeze from beneath her tightly closed eyelids. 'It – it just happened.'

'Then make sure it doesn't happen again.'

There was another awful pause, and then the pressure

increased in her rear passage and she felt the inanimate object sink into her. Her back arched involuntarily.

'Good girl,' he encouraged firmly. 'Now hold still.'

Selina held her breath, anticipating his next move. Gradually he slid the violating object in and out of her lubricated rectum and skewered it in small circles. Now Selina understood why Kim had ultimately relished the same treatment, because sensations the like of which she'd never dreamed of before were building in the pit of her stomach. Her legs trembled and threatened to give way. The breath caught in her lungs and her breasts swelled against the table as she gasped for air, and her hips began to grind back towards the beautiful cylinder that was stretching and filling her with exquisite bliss.

'Yesss… yesss…' she mumbled, salty tears on her lips. 'Please… I'm coming…'

Oliver intensified the movements. It was all too much for Selina's tormented body. Her back dipped and arched, and throwing her head back, her lustrous hair sweeping her shoulders, she stiffened and came with a long groan.

She remained motionless for long seconds, statuesque on her elbows and taut legs, her erect nipples gently swaying against the cold table, and then she slumped limply and lay quiet, her shoulders moving gently as her breathing calmed.

So replete was Selina, she barely noticed her surroundings any longer. She was vaguely aware of movement and rustlings behind her, and Oliver saying something about it being his turn. There was a chink of metal and then she felt the leather straps being folded across her back and the buckles being tightened, but she had no energy, or any real will, with which to resist.

Strong hands, certainly Oliver's, caressed the cheeks of her bottom, and then prised them apart. More cool gel was gently massaged into her tender entrance. Her sphincter tightened as a finger wriggled inside, but still she did nothing to deny it.

The rude digit disappeared, and then something much larger and smooth pressed into the deep valley between her buttocks and demanded entry into her rear passage. Selina became more aware of what was happening, but before she could do or say anything Oliver lunged with his hips and his huge erection forged its way into her clutching depths.

The leather belts creaked as Selina stiffened and tried to squirm away, but it was hopeless, and she could do nothing but lay there, impaled to the table beneath Oliver's weight.

'Bloody hell, that feels good!' panted Oliver, his staccato breath ruffling the silky hair at her temple. His large hands gripped the edge of the table by her disbelieving face, he lowered himself and covered her back, and started to rhythmically lever himself against her immobilised body. Selina knew another orgasm was fast approaching, and she tried her best to grind back against the humid groin that enveloped her stretched bottom. As the ecstasy of the perverse coupling overwhelmed her she felt the living shaft pulse and then her bottom was filled with his scolding seed. She abandoned herself to the dark delights he was teaching her to embrace. Oliver grunted and filled her again, and then he slumped down, his head lolling beside hers, his slack jaw on her perspiring shoulder.

'That'll do for now,' he eventually sighed as he stood up and moved away.

Georgina moved in with a devilish look on her face and released their victim. She helped the exhausted girl to stand, turned her, and as Selina leant her abused bottom against the table Georgina swooped and kissed her, her tongue passionately invading the startled girl's mouth.

'Please… please no more,' Selina breathed when the consuming kiss finally ended. But Georgina ignored her and pinched her still-erect nipples. Then she lowered her head and sucked one into her mouth. Selina sighed, and couldn't resist arching her back and feeding more of her breast into that warm moist haven. Through fluttering lashes she saw Oliver watching them as he pulled up his trousers and tucked his shirt in, and then she wailed and writhed as sharp teeth sank into her poor nipple. The pain was intense, and she frantically tried to extricate herself from the devious woman's clutches. But despite her horror she felt her juices start to flow again as the woman continued to gnaw on her poor bud like a determined puppy. Inexplicably, yet another orgasm was building. For a second Selina despised her own weak lasciviousness, but the pleasure and pain was simply too much to deny. She came again, and before she could recover Georgina had released her and left her alone, a pitiful creature slouched and sobbing against the table, with one of the other three occupants of the room studying her with pity in her eyes, and two of them with amusement in theirs.

Once back in the main house Oliver became brisk and businesslike again, as though nothing at all had just occurred.

'I'd like my breakfast at eight-thirty,' he said curtly to Selina, before handing her a piece of folded paper. 'Set your alarm for seven and don't dress until you've been along to my room. Here's a list of my requirements for tomorrow. They shouldn't prove too arduous for you, but if you make any mistakes you will of course be punished. You have terminated your staff's employment, I trust?'

'No, I haven't,' said Selina apologetically. 'I keep putting it off.'

'Then tell them tonight before you go to bed,' Oliver ordered. 'I want them gone after breakfast. There must be no one around us apart from Kim over the next few days. Later in the week we'll be joined by my own staff, but they're quite used to my ways.'

Selina didn't want to think too much about what he was telling her. The realisation that his indoctrination of her had only just begun was disturbing enough, but even more so was the fact that she knew, despite what had happened to her that evening, that she had reached a greater pinnacle of pleasure than ever before. Somehow, from the moment he had set eyes on her, Oliver had seen what kind of a girl she was and had known that she would take pleasure from the things he enjoyed. No matter how many humiliations were heaped upon her she continued to feel more and more alive, and she wondered how she could have believed she even existed before he'd taken over as owner of Summerfield Hall.

As she forced herself to pick up the phone and inform the staff that they were no longer required, she realised that this wasn't the worst thing she had to do that night. The worst thing was facing up to the truth about herself, and the fact that even now she was excited by the prospect of what lay ahead. Her excitement was all the more extraordinary because she lived in a perpetual state of fear, terrified of annoying or disobeying the charismatic Oliver Richards. And yet – perversely – even more exciting was the way her treacherous body would then start to tense in anticipation of some forbidden excitement, some dark pain-filled punishment that would end in a paroxysm of pleasure so intense that that too was a strange kind of pain.

She was grateful that her father had no idea what was happening to her.

Chapter Six

As soon as Selina's alarm went off the next morning she hurried into the bathroom for a quick shower. She cleaned her teeth, put on her bathrobe, and then left her room and padded along the landing. Taking a deep breath and collecting her thoughts, she knocked lightly on Oliver's door.

'I'm glad to see you were up on time,' he remarked, opening the door and brusquely beckoning her inside. He smiled in amusement at her robe, and swiftly undid the tie at her waist and slipped it off her.

'That's better, my dear,' he said. 'No need to be so coy.'

Selina wondered why, despite all the liberties he'd already taken with her, she still felt incredibly shy when standing naked in front of him. His eyes always seemed to be searching her body in such a strange manner, as though looking for something new, something he'd missed on previous inspections.

'Stay where you are,' he said, 'but spread your feet apart a little.'

Hastily she obeyed, remembering his threat of the night before and not wishing to be punished so early in the morning.

From his pocket he took a small silver tube and a latex glove. She watched, dumbfounded, as he snapped on the glove like a surgeon preparing for an operation, removed the top of the tube, and squeezed a little of the cream onto his index finger.

'This wondrous substance can only be found in certain

magical areas of the Orient,' he explained, seeing the look of puzzlement on Selina's face. 'It makes the skin incredibly sensitive, which is why I don't want it on my finger. As you can imagine, it will greatly enhance your pleasure, but it also means you will yearn for pleasure even more.

'I'm going to apply some now, and then dress you appropriately,' he continued matter-of-factly. 'As a result you will doubtless find that your body is constantly stimulated. You'll feel as though you're perched on the edge of an orgasm if anything so much as brushes against you, and you should have many climaxes during the day – but I don't want them to be too visible. The idea of this lesson is for you to acquire the ability to conceal your pleasure. Kim is already very capable at that. You can watch her for guidance if you find it too difficult. No doubt your moments of extreme rapture will be obvious to me at first, but by the end of the day I expect to see few outward signs. Do you understand me?'

His words both excited and worried Selina, but she nodded.

Looking satisfied with her response, Oliver reached out and applied the innocuous-looking blob to both her nipples and the surrounding areolae, before crouching down, parting her sex lips, and coating a slick of it on her clitoris. Then, to her consternation, he straightened up and pressed between her shoulders, and as she bent forward he dabbed some of the cream between the cheeks of her bottom, finally inserting the index finger just inside the puckered entrance.

By this time the ointment was already affecting her nipples. They burned slightly, feeling tingly and hot. They were already erect and sending frantic messages of need to the rest of her body. Between her thighs the sensation was even worse. It was as though incredibly skilful fingers were slowly teasing her, and she could feel how moist she was

83

already becoming. To her horror she realised that the same feelings were simmering in her rectum, warming and arousing at the same time.

'Now for the clothing,' said Oliver, watching with interest as Selina squirmed in front of him, shifting restlessly from one foot to the other, fighting the temptation to touch herself and release her rising passions. Opening his right hand she saw what looked like a tiny plastic plug lying in the palm.

'What's that?' she asked.

'It's an anal plug,' he said calmly. 'It should be very effective since I've put some ointment in there. Bend over quickly now, it's nearly time for my breakfast.'

She didn't dare disobey, although she couldn't imagine how she was going to get through the day since her body seemed to be on fire. As he slid the small rounded plug into her rectum she was horrified to realise that she was about to come, and then she was shuddering and shaking as the ointment had its insidious way with her.

'It seems it's effective enough,' said Oliver dryly. 'Mind you, you'd have to be blind not to have seen you come then. I'll forgive you though, as it was your first time.'

'This is wicked,' exclaimed Selina. 'How can you do this to me? I'm going to be turned on all day.'

'Of course you are, that's the idea,' said Oliver smugly. 'If you weren't, how would you learn to disguise it?'

He then proceeded to dress Selina in a skimpy leather bikini bra, and a tight pair of leather briefs with an open crotch and a thong that fitted snugly between her buttocks and kept the anal plug in place. She'd never worn leather before, nor had her breasts ever felt quite so constrained as they were by the revealing garment.

'Just touch the tip of your right nipple for a moment,' said Oliver thoughtfully, and Selina was quick to obey because it was what she most wanted to do. But even she was horrified when the moment her finger touched the flesh, so over-excited by the strange ointment from the Orient, she once more spasmed in release of a tiny orgasm.

'You didn't hide that one any better,' remarked Oliver. 'I think I'll add a little more ointment.'

'No, please don't!' the poor girl gasped. 'I couldn't bear any more. I promise I'll try harder next time.'

'That's your last chance,' said Oliver ominously, and then he held out what looked like one of his own shirts for her to put her arms into. It was crisp and white, with a thin grey stripe running through it, and he slipped it over her shoulders and then fastened a few buttons at the bottom. This meant that the upper slopes of her breasts, thrust forward by the leather bra, were fully exposed, and the hem of the shirt only just covered her buttocks.

'I can't walk around like this,' she protested.

'The servants will be gone soon. And Georgina returned to London last night, so only Kim and I will be here to see you,' Oliver reminded her.

'But what if they see me before they go?' asked Selina despairingly.

'Then it will give them something to talk about in the village, won't it?' he scoffed. 'I'm going downstairs now,' he added, 'I want my breakfast.'

After he had left her alone she saw he'd left a pair of black stiletto shoes for her to wear. She slipped into them and hurried awkwardly down the wide staircase to the main hall, praying that none of the servants saw her, so clearly the sexual plaything of the new owner of Summerfield Hall.

She was unlucky. Riley the long-serving gardener was just collecting his pay from Oliver, and he stared up at her in astonishment, his mouth hanging open but his eyes devouring her.

So embarrassed was Selina that she nearly stumbled, and had to grip the banister tightly. She wanted to hang her head in shame but knew that Oliver would be angry with her if she did. With an effort she held it defiantly high, walked past the startled Riley, and along the corridor to the kitchen. She knew full well that both he and Oliver would be watching every step she took, and as she walked the tight leather thong pressed the anal butt ever more firmly into her rectum and the nerve-endings there, constantly over-stimulated by the potent ointment, suddenly reacted by sending an orgasm rippling through her. The exquisite sensations took her totally by surprise. She gasped and then stood for a moment, trembling until the pleasure ebbed.

Once the moment passed she hurried into the kitchen and began seeing to the breakfast things. Kim was already there. She was dressed exactly the same as Selina, only her shirt was red with white stripes and the leather bra beneath was also red. Her normally tiny nipples were fully extended and clearly pressing through the shirt. Selina could imagine how the other girl was feeling, but she didn't dare say anything, because Kim refused to meet her eyes and busied herself making the coffee.

When Oliver rang the two girls hurried through to the dining room, Selina carrying the plate of scrambled egg, grilled bacon and toast, while Kim followed with a silver tray bearing the coffee pot, cream, and coffee cup and saucer.

Oliver watched them both closely. 'That was a disgraceful exhibition you made of yourself just now,' he said to Selina. 'You promised me the next time you came you were going to make some effort to disguise it.'

'I didn't know I was going to come,' explained Selina, miserably. 'It just swept over me.'

'That's no excuse,' he retorted. 'I'm afraid I shall have

to punish you after I've eaten.' He turned to the Oriental girl. 'Come here, Kim.'

The slim-hipped girl walked towards her new master, but Selina could see that whereas when he looked at her it was always with keen interest, there was total indifference in his eyes when he surveyed Georgina's toy. Languidly he reached inside the red shirt and cupped one of the small leather-encased breasts, moving it up and down, increasing the stimulation of the ointment. Kim's eyes grew wide as Oliver continued to jiggle her breast, and then she clenched her teeth tightly together. Selina watched in fascination as Kim breathed slowly. She stood rigid and motionless as tiny beads of perspiration appeared on her forehead and top lip, but not a single muscle moved, and after a few seconds Oliver removed his hand, glancing up at Selina.

'You see what I mean?' he said shortly. 'You came then, didn't you Kim?'

'Yes sir,' the young beauty confirmed.

'By the end of the day I expect you to remain as statuesque as she did,' said Oliver, and Selina shook her head in disbelief.

'I don't think I can,' she whispered. 'She must have had a lot more practice than just one day.'

'You're on the fast learning track,' he said. 'We don't have that much time. Anyway, it's more fun done like this. I expect Christian took weeks, but then he takes nearly that long to sum up for a jury!' He chuckled to himself, and Selina realised that Kim had told the truth; he certainly didn't seem to care too much for Christian Wells.

After he'd eaten the girls removed the dishes. Selina was quickly learning that no matter what movement she made, the material of the shirt would move as well and was continually brushing against her permanently aroused nipples, or else she would have to bend and the anal plug would be pressed more tightly inside her. Every time this happened she'd experience a tiny orgasm and her muscles would ripple in a shameful way, revealing her pleasure.

'How do you think he'll punish me?' she asked Kim anxiously.

Kim shrugged. 'I don't know his ways. He and Christian are not alike.'

'But will it hurt?' asked Selina.

Kim gave a rare smile. 'Of course it will hurt. That's the point of all this, isn't it?'

'I really don't know any more,' said Selina hopelessly. 'I don't understand what he's doing to me.'

'Whatever he's doing to you, you're choosing to let him,' Kim reminded her.

It wasn't as simple as that, thought Selina. It was all so complex, but she didn't really understand it herself, so how could she expect Kim to?

Later, as Selina was dusting and trying desperately to prevent the muscles of her belly from convulsing as yet another small climax washed over her, Oliver walked into the room.

'Turn round,' he commanded her. He looked at her flushed face for a moment. 'You look as though you're trying hard,' he remarked, and then he reached down and to her horror she felt his fingers probing through the open crotch of the leather thong.

'Please don't touch me there,' she begged him. 'It all feels so...'

'So what?' he asked her intently. 'Describe it to me. Tell me how you feel, Selina.'

'It's burning,' she said pathetically. 'I feel hot, puffy and damp. It's as though all I need is one tiny touch and I shall come and never be able to stop coming.'

'That would be an interesting phenomenon,' said Oliver.

'Now I can't possibly resist testing your theory out.'

'Don't! Don't I beg you,' Selina sobbed, knowing that if he touched her there the climax would be far more intense and she'd never be able to conceal it.

Oliver was unmoved by her cries, and his fingers probed knowingly. Immediately she felt the gathering together of muscles, the bunching and tightening, the coiling – sensations so blissful and yet so terrifying because of the restraints imposed upon her.

Then, in an act of fiendish cruelty, Oliver swirled his finger against her protruding clitoris and just as Selina had feared, an enormous orgasm exploded deep within her belly. She groaned as her muscles contracted and for minute after endless minute her pleasure refused to end until it became a kind of delicious torment.

She struggled to subdue it, to force the wrenching muscles to be still and to stop herself from throwing back her head and screaming her delight, but it was impossible. The pleasure was simply too great. When he finally removed his fingers her body continued to take pleasure, the ointment somehow providing enough stimulation on its own so that still she could not stand motionless for him and he waited impatiently, his fingers tapping the sides of his legs, for her to regain control.

At last it was over, and she slowly opened her misty eyes and refocused on her surroundings.

'About time,' said Oliver. 'I have to say that you've disappointed me, Selina. Luckily I already had a punishment prepared for you. I had wondered if it was too severe, but after such flagrant disobedience it's clear it isn't. You do ride, I hope?'

'Oh yes,' said Selina innocently, her voice husky with emotion. 'I learnt when I was about six.'

'Good. Then we're both going for a ride. And on that

ride you will learn to disguise your pleasure once and for all. It is vital that you succeed.'

'But I don't know how to do it,' explained Selina, starting to cry. 'Wuh – what am I meant to do?'

'I suggest you ask Kim,' he said. 'I'll collect you from the side entrance in ten minutes. Incidentally, don't bother to change, except for your shoes of course. You may put on some riding boots.'

Selina hurried to the small utility room off the kitchen where boots and outdoor clothing were kept. She was relieved to meet Kim in the hallway, and grabbing her by the arm, pulled her along. 'Quickly,' she exclaimed as she gathered a pair of boots and sat on a kitchen bench to pull them on, wincing as the anal butt pushed more firmly into her poor bottom. 'Tell me what I must do to stop him from seeing when I'm coming.'

'It isn't easy,' said the other girl. 'It takes a lot of training.'

'You must give me some advice,' Selina begged. 'If you don't, I dread to think how long I'm going to be out there.'

'Always breathe slowly through your mouth, but without making it obvious,' whispered Kim. 'Also, I tighten my muscles when I feel an orgasm coming and press downwards. It helps to disguise it. You can always change position when you feel the contractions sweeping through you. Change position naturally that is, as though you're just readjusting yourself or resettling. The trouble is,' she added, 'all this means that the orgasms are never complete, and the tension builds so that afterwards you feel as though you haven't come at all. Georgina never lets me have an orgasm at the end where I can just let go. Sometimes I can't sleep for the aching in my breasts and between my thighs, when she's played that particular game with me.'

'Why are they so cruel to us?' asked Selina.

'Because we're honoured.'

Selina stared at her for a moment trying to understand her meaning, but then she heard the sound of horse's hooves outside and hurried to meet Oliver.

To her surprise he had only brought one horse round to the side entrance, a large chestnut mare, one of the two horses her father had managed to keep on at Summerfield Hall even when his money started to disappear.

'Aren't you riding?' she asked.

'No, I'm going to put you on a lunging rein,' he explained.

'But I don't need a lunging rein – I'm a very accomplished horsewoman.'

'I'm sure you are, but this will be something completely new for you,' said Oliver, ominously. 'Put your foot in the stirrup and climb on.'

As she lifted one leg to the stirrup he reached beneath her to make sure that the sides around the open crotch of her leather panties were pulled as far apart as possible.

'Go ahead,' he said curtly, when satisfied.

Selina swung herself into the saddle and then stopped, looking down at the gleaming leather in surprise. This wasn't her usual saddle. This was something new. Towards the front of it, shining wickedly in the summer sun, was a polished leather protrusion of about four inches in length, tapering and angled.

'That fits inside you,' Oliver casually explained.

Selina hesitated. Already, due to the insidious arousal of the strange ointment, her sex was swollen and tingling and driving her into a frenzy. She knew that if she did as she was told she would climax within seconds, and then as she glanced at Oliver's face she realised that was exactly his intention. Somehow she had to try and hide the climax from him.

Slowly and hesitantly she did as he ordered, feeling the cool polished surface of the strange leather prong sliding easily inside her already moist and aroused entrance. And then, as she settled her full weight into the saddle, the shaped tip brushed against the front of her upper vaginal wall, which meant that her G-spot would be under permanent pressure.

'I found a small paddock at the back of the old wing of the house,' remarked Oliver. 'I think we'll go there.'

Grasping the horse's reins he led it along the gravel path around the back of the house, over the bridge, and then round into the paddock where Selina had once practiced as a child on her very first pony. During that short walk she realised exactly what she was in for. Despite the fact that they were going so slowly, the constant rolling and pitching meant that the anal butt and the stimulator on the saddle were moving all the time, tantalising her inner-most flesh. The shirt, too, fluttered in the morning breeze and brushed constantly against her over-excited nipples.

Selina tried to remember Kim's advice. As they reached the edge of the paddock she knew her first orgasm was imminent and breathed very slowly through slightly parted lips. Then, when the contractions began, she determinedly tightened her stomach muscles and bore down, feeling certain she'd given no sign of what had occurred.

Oliver glanced up at her suddenly flushed face. Swiftly he pulled the hem of her shirt up so he could study her flat tummy, but there was no movement there and he realised he'd missed the moment.

'Congratulations,' he said. 'I think it would be better if you took the shirt off now. The sun's warm, no doubt you'll enjoy the feel of it on your skin.'

Selina knew then that he was determined to make her ordeal as difficult for her as possible. Without the protection of the shirt some movement was bound to show in her belly, if not her breasts. But she obeyed, dropping the garment to the ground.

'Now I'm going to fix the lunging rein,' Oliver informed her. 'You probably learnt like that as a child.' Selina nodded. 'Good. Start the horse walking in large circles in a clockwise direction, and only use your knees. Fold your hands behind the back of your neck, it will strengthen your thigh muscles.'

That wasn't all it did. It meant that Selina's leather-encased breasts jutted forward and up as she arched her back in order to keep her balance, and when she gripped tightly with her thigh muscles everything inside her tightened as well. To her horror, without any warning at all, the insistent pulse began to throb behind her nub of pleasure, and she realised she was going to come again, only seconds after her first climax. This time it was positively painful to press down against the surging muscles as they attempted to ripple and spasm in order to gain full release, but she was quite determined not to let anything show. To her relief the gentle wave of pleasure passed through her without any visible signs, although when it was gone she knew that Kim had been right, because she still felt as though she needed an orgasm, and not as though her pleasure had already spilled over.

Oliver watched her intently, obviously realising that somehow she must be managing to hide her pleasure from him, and although this was what he'd wanted, he seemed angry that she'd learned so quickly.

'Trot on,' he said to the horse. Instantly it obeyed, and now Selina was rising and falling in the saddle, the tortuous leather prong stabbing in and out of her, and every time she fell the anal butt stimulated her rectum. At the same time the rapid movement of her breasts meant that her nipples, constantly smarting and swollen from the ointment, began to send their own signals down between her ribs deep into her belly, where once more the coiling sensation was beginning.

Because of the increase in the horse's speed all the sensations were increased ten-fold, and she felt as though her entire body would explode. She felt the hot flush of arousal rising through her, and this time the spasming muscles would not be subdued, and as she came the delicious flooding sensation made her gasp, and she knew her whole body was shaking.

'Pull up,' snapped Oliver.

Quickly she brought the horse to a standstill.

'You came then, didn't you?' he accused.

Selina nodded.

'Did you try and hide it?'

Again she nodded, aware that he must know how well she'd already done, but he gave no sign of appreciation. Instead he lifted her roughly off the horse and manhandled her across the paddock until she was facing the white fence that surrounded it.

She was totally unprepared for the shock of the riding crop. It snaked around her waist, biting cruelly into her still trembling flesh. Then as it uncurled and she drew a sigh of relief, Oliver struck again, only this time higher so that the tip of the crop caught her engorged nipples. To her shame this triggered yet another frantic spasm that she wrestled to conceal, pressing against the upward contractions with all her might, leaning slightly forward over the fence as Kim had suggested, in order to hide any telltale signs.

'Clever,' said Oliver approvingly. He possessively tweaked each of the sore nipples in turn, and then very slowly rolled them between his fingertips until she gave a moan of pleasure. Luckily for her, her body was too exhausted by the three orgasms she'd already received for her to come again, and all she had was the pleasure of the caress.

'Back on the horse,' he said, abruptly releasing her.

And then it was back to the same torment, a torment that continued for two hours as he put the horse through its paces and Selina tried, sometimes successfully, sometimes not, to hide every shattering climax that the movement of the animal beneath her caused.

Finally Oliver seemed to decide that she'd learnt enough, because he removed the lunging rein and began to lead the horse back to the house, allowing Selina to walk alongside him. He glanced down at her. 'You did better than I expected,' he said approvingly. 'Did Kim give you some advice?'

'Yes,' admitted Selina.

'And how do you feel now?' he asked with interest.

Selina brushed her hair back off her damp forehead. She didn't want to tell him, but if she lied she was certain he would know. 'I'm still aroused,' she admitted in shame. 'It doesn't feel as though I've come at all.'

'It never does when you have to control it to such an extent,' explained Oliver, echoing what Kim had said earlier. 'That's why it's a punishment. It's more than that though; I like my friends to see how well my girl's can control themselves. It's a trick that always impresses them.'

'But how will they know?' asked Selina, puzzled.

'Because I shall make you come in front of them and tell you to conceal it,' he explained, in a matter-of-fact manner.

Selina looked up at him in astonishment. 'I wouldn't be able to come if strangers were watching me,' she whispered.

'Rubbish,' he said. 'Georgina and Kim haven't put you off, at least not as far as I've noticed.'

'That's different,' protested Selina. 'They've been here almost from the beginning. I couldn't just perform like a

95

party entertainer.'

'That's exactly what you will be doing, my dear,' said Oliver. 'And very soon too, if I have my way. There are just a few more things for you to learn, and then you should be ready for a dinner party in London.

'Ah, good,' he added, and Selina followed his gaze. 'It looks as though some of my staff are arriving.'

Selina tried to hide behind him. She didn't want the new staff to see her dressed like that, wearing only long riding boots, a leather thong, a leather open-cup bra, and Oliver's shirt thrown casually over her shoulders. If they did they'd never have any respect for her.

Oliver gripped her by the shoulder and pushed her in front of him. 'Where do you think you're going?' he asked. 'It's time for you to meet them.'

Mortified and scarlet with shame, Selina was hustled round to the side door where two cars were drawing up. 'Lift your head up and stand proudly,' Oliver ordered her. 'Remember, they know you're my mistress and they'll expect you to give them some orders. I don't expect you to show any shame.'

Three people climbed out of the cars. The first was a woman in her mid-fifties with grey hair cut in a short severe style. 'This is Mrs Soames,' said Oliver, as the woman approached. 'She's my housekeeper, and has been for the past ten years. Mrs Soames, I'd like you to meet Selina.'

The woman held out a hand, looking Selina straight in the eyes, apparently quite unaffected by her extraordinary outfit. 'I'm delighted to meet you, miss,' she said politely.

'And this,' continued Oliver, 'is Jake. Jake is my personal manservant. He also acts as handyman and chauffeur, so he's kept fairly busy.'

Jake seemed as unaffected as Mrs Soames by Selina's appearance, but she was very affected by his. He was several inches shorter than Oliver and had long fair hair. But it was clear from his tight fitting jeans and white T-shirt that he was well built, and it looked as though he worked out. He was also quite young, only about twenty-two or twenty-three, which made it doubly shaming for Selina.

'And finally, I'd like you to meet Mary,' said Oliver. 'Mary will act as your personal maid.'

'But I don't need a personal maid,' replied Selina.

'I'll decide what you do and what you don't need,' Oliver snapped coldly. 'Mary's very good at her duties and will be a great help, both to you and to me. Besides, she and Jake go everywhere together.'

When Selina shook hands with Mary she sensed antagonism from the sullen girl.

Mary was probably only a year or so older than Selina, but she had a knowing look in her slightly slanted green eyes, and her red hair, which was pulled harshly back off her face, was thick and shining. There was something very sexual about her; a sexuality that made Selina feel uneasy, and unlike the other two servants, Mary was clearly amused by what Selina was wearing. She was the last person on earth Selina would have chosen as a personal maid, but Oliver had given her no choice, and she knew very well that he must have his own reasons.

'Has Georgina told you all what the sleeping arrangements will be?' asked Oliver.

'Yes, thank you sir,' replied Mrs Soames, and the three of them disappeared into the side entrance.

'Does Mrs Soames do the cooking too?' enquired Selina.

Oliver nodded. 'You'll be amazed how much she does,' he said. 'The only reason she's remained with me for so long is that she manages to keep up with my demands. She's highly paid of course, but worth every penny.

'And as for Mary… well, let's just say that having Mary around should prove very interesting, and I'm looking forward to seeing how the pair of you get on.'

'I still can't imagine why I'll need her.'

'You'll find,' said Oliver, 'that there will be times in the future when – at the most inappropriate moments – you decide to resist me. Mary will always be there to make sure that these little awkward moments are smoothed over. She knows that when I have guests I don't like anything to go wrong, and she'll quickly get used to you and know what to do should you prove difficult.'

'I thought that if I didn't want to do what you asked I was free to go,' said Selina, suddenly feeling somewhat anxious again.

'Of course you can go,' Oliver repeated. 'But I'm sure your father taught you it was bad manners to leave in the middle of a dinner party. Mary's only there for that kind of emergency. Of course, she also helps you get ready for bed at night.' For some reason this seemed to amuse him, and with a smile he led the horse away, leaving Selina to go back into the house on her own.

'Oliver,' she called uncertainly. He turned his head in surprise. 'I just wondered how long the effects of this ointment will last? I still feel so...'

'Yes,' he said, 'I can imagine. I seem to remember it's about four hours. By late afternoon I imagine things will be calming down for you. Incidentally, if you do have any more orgasms before then, you don't have to hide them. I think you've learned your lesson well enough.'

Feeling shattered by the events of the morning, Selina hurried up to her room, anxious to change. But there, already waiting for her, she found Mary. It was then that Selina realised how difficult privacy was going to be in the future. Clearly Oliver liked to have her watched all the time, and since it wasn't possible for him to always be with her, Mary was to take his place in the intimacy of her bedroom.

'I've come to change. I don't need you,' she told the auburn girl.

'I have some clothes ready for you,' said Mary, and there was a note of contempt in her voice.

'But I haven't decided what I want to wear yet.'

'I know what Mr Richards would want you to wear,' the maid said confidently, and she produced a long canary-yellow jersey-dress.

For some reason Selina didn't dare argue, but she couldn't help sighing with relief as she eased off the leather bra and her breasts burst free of the tight restraint. She decided to leave the tiny leather panties on, feeling it offered some support to the anal plug that still tormented her so wickedly.

She slipped the jersey dress over her head and immediately the fabric clung to her like a second skin. The tantalising contact with her aching nipples proved fatal, and she was suddenly overwhelmed by yet another sweet orgasm, more gentle than some she'd experienced earlier, but still a blissful release from the perpetual needs of her body. She trembled, crying out softly, acutely aware that she no longer had to control herself, and it was only when the moment had passed and her body was briefly at rest that she realised Mary was watching with her piercing green eyes.

'I chose well,' said the girl, and Selina quickly slipped her feet into a pair of beige open-toed sandals and walked unsteadily from the room.

When Selina finally went to bed that night she was exhausted. Once she'd changed into the yellow dress after her horse riding she'd spent most of the day showing Mrs

Soames around the kitchen and dining area of Summerfield Hall. Many times she'd had to bend or stretch, twist or turn in order to open cupboard doors or show the new housekeeper where things were kept, and she lost count of the number of orgasms she had due to the relentless stimulation of her permanently aroused flesh.

However, as the afternoon wore on so the orgasms had decreased in number and intensity, and she realised Oliver had told her the truth. By four o'clock the effects of the ointment had finally worn off and, after her initial relief, she found that in a strange way she missed the perpetual titillation it had given her. Even so, she knew that no one could be continually stimulated and that the break was necessary.

As she went to her bedroom her only desire was for a good night's sleep, and so she was less than pleased to find Mary waiting for her. 'What do you want?' she demanded.

'I've run you a bath,' explained the girl.

Selina pulled off the yellow dress and finally removed the leather thong. As she bent over to step out of it she was startled to feel a touch on her buttocks and a sudden twisting sensation in her rectum, and she nearly died as she spun round and saw Mary holding the anal plug.

'I'll dispose of this for you ma'am,' the girl said politely, the laughter in her eyes scarcely concealed.

'H-how did you know it was there?' demanded Selina.

'I've seen it all before. I've worked for Mr Richards for two years now. I'm well used to his ways.'

Selina didn't wish to pursue that line of conversation and padded through into the bathroom, which was filled with steam and the aroma of some lightly scented bath oil. 'You don't need to follow me in here,' she snapped, realising Mary was behind her.

'But I have to help you wash,' explained the girl.

'Who said?' asked Selina, but she already knew the answer to that.

'Mr Richards, of course,' Mary replied. 'I answer only to him.'

As Selina slid into the deliciously warm water, Mary bent over her and began to lather her back, neck and breasts with a soapy sponge. Despite her irritation at the other girl's presence, Selina couldn't help but relax, and she rested her head back against the end of the bath, closing her eyes as the tensions of the bizarre day eased out of her. It was only when Mary attempted to wash between her thighs that Selina decided it was time to put her foot down.

'I can do that myself,' she said firmly.

'But I have to,' said Mary in surprise.

'I don't believe you!'

For a few tense seconds there was an impasse, and then clearly realising that Selina wasn't going to change her mind, Mary stormed from the steamy room.

When Selina was finally dried and back in the bedroom Mary silently handed her a long silk camisole top. 'For you to wear tonight,' she said sulkily, and then left the room before Selina could argue yet again.

Alone at last, Selina gave a sigh of relief, climbed onto her bed, and slipped between the cool sheets. Her body, soothed by the bath, was more than ready for sleep, and closing her eyes she swiftly drifted off.

She wasn't sure how long she'd been sleeping before she was woken, but she sensed it had been several hours, and the room was very dark. She could hear the sound of someone breathing close at hand, and gingerly reaching out she snapped on her bedside light.

Oliver was standing over her, wearing a knee-length silk robe belted with a sash.

'I'd hoped to get into bed without you waking,' he

murmured. 'Never mind.' Untying the sash he threw the robe carelessly over a bedside chair, and slipped in beside her.

Selina was astounded. Never in her wildest dreams had she imagined him coming to her at night, and she couldn't think what he wanted from her at such an hour.

'Mary tells me you wouldn't let her obey one of my orders,' he whispered in her ear.

'I didn't believe it was one of your orders,' she explained, trying to clear her foggy brain.

'Well it was, but I'll let you off this time,' he said quietly, as his hands moved over her body, sliding up beneath the hip-length camisole and caressing every inch of her perfumed breasts.

After a few minutes the unwelcome tension his arrival had caused began to ease from her. Instead, a different sort of tension stirred as her eager body sensed it was to experience yet more wicked pleasure.

Oliver suddenly rolled on top of Selina and she could feel his hard cock pressing against her lower belly. For a few moments it remained there while his fingers busied themselves with her treacherous nipples, nipping and squeezing at them as she softly mewed with delight. Then his large hands moved lower again. He parted her thighs and without any further preliminaries pushed himself inside her.

She was ashamed at how easy the entry was for him, realising that as soon as he'd started touching her tender nipples her juices had started to flow and she was now extremely wet. Once inside her he lifted himself up and pulled her with him. Then, when he was kneeling, he grasped her around the tops of her thighs and told her to lower her shoulders back onto the bed. She slowly obeyed, her mouth gaping as she felt him penetrate her further, and then stared up at him with wide sparkling eyes. His own were in shadow and unfathomable. It was impossible to tell how much pleasure he was gaining, but for her the delicious fullness inside what had been an aching void for so much of the day was sheer bliss. Reaching for him she placed her hands on his sturdy thighs and tried to move gently back and forth.

'Keep still,' he said sharply. 'If you want to do anything, put your feet against my chest and use them to caress me.'

Selina needed no second bidding. Immediately her tiny feet were moving across his chest, the toes trailing through the dark hairs. And then she moved them faster and across his nipples, which promptly hardened into little points.

Slowly Oliver leaned back until his erection was pressing against the top inside area of her vagina, and a gorgeous gentle aching started to radiate from her G-spot. Although she wanted to move, Oliver's restraining hands prevented her.

'Keep absolutely still,' he urged. 'Just lie there and wait. Your pleasure will come.'

Selina found that hard to believe, but she obediently remained motionless while Oliver continued to lean back. The pressure remained constant, and gradually the sweet piercing pleasure increased, spreading upwards like an incoming tide until she felt herself tightening around him as her belly began to quake. The delicious pulsating began and her head rolled from side to side as the sweet moment of release grew inexorably nearer. And then her toes, which were still caressing his chest, clenched, and she knew she was only seconds away from orgasm.

'Caress your breasts,' Oliver urged. Selina obeyed instantly because they were desperate for some form of stimulation. Quickly her nimble fingers moved over the rapidly tightening globes until they located the highly sensitive nipples, and then she rolled them between her fingers as Oliver had done earlier.

Now the pleasure seemed to be coming from everywhere. Despite the fact that Oliver was no longer moving, his cock seemed to grow harder and larger within her. The incredible sensations multiplied, and then at last with a scream of excitement she was suffused by yet another wonderful orgasm. She was no longer able to keep still. Her perspiring breasts shimmered in the darkness and her buttocks writhed in his lap, and it was only Oliver's restraining hands that pinned her in place so he could remain embedded in her clutching sex, keeping their mutual pleasure boiling for as long as possible.

When it was over she whimpered weakly, because she'd wanted the blissful moment to continue for even longer. She expected Oliver to withdraw, but then he was manoeuvring her around the bed until she was sitting on top of him, leaning back against his raised knees with her own planted on each side of his waist. In this position his rearing erection penetrated deeper than it had ever penetrated before, and without being given permission she started to play with her breasts. She squeezed her nipples hard in order to savour the pain; a pain she was beginning to crave more and more in order to gain full satisfaction.

At the same time Oliver had his hands free to finger her squelching sex. His touch was no longer light and gentle but almost harsh as his fingertips moved rapidly around the moist flesh beneath her clitoris. It tipped Selina over the edge, and she bucked wildly as colours exploded in her head and a sharp climax tore through her. She began to milk him, and through swirling mists she heard him grunt. As she slumped breathlessly back against his thighs the flesh of her inner sex lips felt sore, but his hands were remorselessly attempting to rekindle her desires.

'Please… please don't,' she begged. 'It's too painful. Let me have just a brief rest.'

But as usual her wishes were of no importance to Oliver. He pushed back the tiny hood of protective flesh covering her retreating clitoris and then, grasping the tiny stem between forefinger and thumb, he began to squeeze just as he had squeezed her nipples in the past, only this time the pain was far more excruciating. It had a different quality to it. It was sharper and keener, cutting like a knife, and Selina was certain she couldn't withstand the torment.

'You're hurting me,' she protested. But he only pinched harder and then, just as she thought she could stand it no longer, the quality of the pain changed and she realised with disbelief that this too was becoming a pleasure. Despite her shame her simmering excitement grew again and she began to writhe beneath his educated fingers.

Oliver ordered her to move up and down on him. 'Lift yourself higher, come down harder,' he muttered through clenched teeth, and every time she slumped back down onto him his massive erection, so hard and thick, hit the back of her cervix, and this extraordinary sensation added to the overall delight.

'Keep clenching yourself around me, contract harder, your muscles should be strong now,' he encouraged. Suddenly, as she struggled to follow his ongoing directions, she felt tiny slivers of excitement spreading from deep inside her moist opening, and realised that these contractions themselves were sending shards of pleasure to join the bitter-sweet pain that he was already causing her.

Then she was coming, twisting and squirming on top of him, and she could feel him erupting inside her, spilling his hot seed and groaning. But even when he was still she continued to gyrate, extracting every last drop of ecstasy so that, for one brief moment, it almost seemed she was using him.

A few minutes later Oliver lifted her as easily as if she was a doll and pulled her down on the bed next to him, her head resting on his chest. His arm was thrown around her, almost an embrace, except that the grip was tight, turning it into a form of imprisonment.

'There's something I have to tell you,' he murmured. 'We're going to London tomorrow for a dinner party. I hadn't wanted to go so soon, you're not really quite ready to meet my friends, but this is important and it was the only day Georgina could arrange for everyone to be there.'

'A dinner party?' queried Selina, her pulse quickening.

'For eight,' said Oliver. 'As it's the first time these people will be meeting you I expect you to be on your best behaviour. You'll do exactly what I say and remember everything I've taught you. Whilst you've been forgiven the odd failure here, I don't expect you to make any in London. If you do, the consequences will be terrible.'

Selina began to tremble. He sounded so serious, and it was only then that she realised that during his stay at Summerfield Hall, despite how severe he'd seemed to her, he was clearly even more frightening in London. 'What will I have to do?' she eventually asked.

'I've no idea,' he said carelessly. 'It depends on what my guests want, and on my mood tomorrow night. We'll be returning the following morning, because you need further training before I can throw a party here at Summerfield Hall.'

'Who will they think I am?' she asked.

'My mistress, naturally. You'll be the hostess for the evening, but don't worry, you only have to look attractive and obey me. Everyone there is used to my dinner parties. Nothing that happens will be new to them, only to you.'

'Does it have to be tomorrow? I don't think I'm ready.'

'In that case you'll have to take your punishment, won't you?' he said through the darkness. 'But you've learnt a lot very quickly. There's no reason why you should fail. Sleep now, we'll be leaving tomorrow morning, at about eleven.'

Despite her exhaustion Selina found it impossible to find sleep for a long time. Whilst what had gone on at Summerfield Hall had been extreme to say the least, the prospect of being paraded and no doubt forced to display her wanton sexuality to strangers was so unsettling that it was only in the early hours that she finally closed her eyes and drifted off.

Her dreams were strange, darkly erotic, and deeply disturbing.

Chapter Seven

As Oliver swung his luxury car out of Summerfield Hall he glanced at Selina sitting in the seat next to him. Secretly he was quite worried about the dinner party that lay ahead. He had a suspicion that Georgina had deliberately brought the date forward because she wanted Selina to fail, although he couldn't for the life of him imagine why. It wasn't as though he and Georgina were lovers, or had ever had a full relationship, and she'd never before displayed any signs of jealousy, but he sensed there was something about Selina that Georgina didn't like.

Just as Georgina apparently wanted Selina to fail, so Oliver desperately wanted her to succeed because, at that moment, she was the most promising girl he'd ever trained. Her incredibly protected upbringing, far from making the task difficult, had made it delightfully easy. He wondered what her father would think if he realised that the years of sensual deprivation he'd inflicted upon her had resulted in such frustration that as soon as she was given an opportunity she'd grasped it with both hands, entering more rapidly and with more enthusiasm into Oliver's dark world than anyone before her.

Not that he was getting overexcited yet. Experience had taught him that girls could fail at the most unlikely of moments, and the memory of Lisette was still fresh in his mind. Nevertheless, her appetite for pleasure and pain and domination seemed to be insatiable. He only hoped that once she was in the presence of other people her inbred inhibitions, caused by her father, would not return to spoil everything.

Next to him Selina was sitting quietly, her hands folded in her lap, and her short skirt had risen up her thighs, the lovely view making him stir with excitement. That excitement wasn't just because he could reach out and touch her legs. It was because he knew that before the start of their journey he'd inserted four vibrating balls inside her vagina, and each ball could throb and pulsate independently, keeping her permanently aroused and on the edge of orgasm. The remote power control was next to him on the driving seat, and he decided to press the button. Because Selina was staring straight ahead, lost in her own thoughts, the sudden movement of the balls took her by surprise. He heard her tiny gasp and tried to imagine how it must feel, sitting on the deep leather seat in the deliciously air-conditioned car, one moment comfortable and the next feeling a powerful surge of desire.

'How do you like my little toy?' he asked.

Selina couldn't reply. Her body was quivering and her cheeks were flushed as she tried desperately to move herself into a less arousing position.

'You're allowed to come,' he reminded her. 'This is just to relax you, to get you in the right mood for the dinner.'

'I know,' gasped Selina, 'but it all exhausts me.'

'I want you to come,' persisted Oliver, 'and I want you to tell me when you're about to.'

Only a few seconds later he was rewarded with another startled gasp from her. 'I'm coming!' she cried. And then she was wriggling ecstatically on her seat, arching her back slightly, and he couldn't resist reaching out and letting his left hand move up her thigh so he could run a finger teasingly around the silken fabric of her panties, already damp with escaping love juices.

Despite Selina's protests he kept her aroused for most of

the journey. Even when they stopped for a coffee at a motorway café he set the balls in motion while she was drinking, and watched as she struggled to remember the lessons learned on horseback at Summerfield Hall; subduing all visible signs of the climax that was racing through her. Only tiny beads of perspiration on her forehead betrayed her, and he nodded approvingly as they left.

'You see how valuable that lesson was now?' he remarked.

Selina didn't answer him.

By the time they arrived at his three-storey Georgian-style townhouse in Belgravia she looked utterly wretched, but at the same time her eyes were shining and her colour high.

'What's the matter?' he asked. 'Why are you looking so unhappy?'

'Because the pleasure's too much,' she explained haltingly. 'You don't know what it's like to have to climax when you don't want to.'

'You enjoy it,' he said dismissively. 'You're obviously as insatiable as your mother was.'

Striding to the front door he rang the bell and his butler, the only member of the staff not to have been moved to Summerfield Hall, opened the door to him.

'Good afternoon, sir,' he said politely, and then he saw Selina standing next to Oliver. 'Good afternoon, madam,' he added.

'This is Selina Swift,' explained Oliver. 'She'll be spending the night with me and acting as hostess for the dinner.'

'Very good sir,' said the butler without batting an eyelid, and then he was moving to the car to collect their cases while Oliver, his eyes checking every room carefully, strode through the house. Selina trailed behind him until at last they were upstairs and in his huge master bedroom with *en suite* bathroom.

'You'd better have a bath and then rest,' he said. 'Our guests are arriving at eight for eight-thirty. Georgina's bringing a friend, so that's someone you'll know. The other four guests are work-related. Christian Wells is another defence lawyer – I'm not sure what his partner does – and Harry is in banking. He's bringing his wife.'

'What am I to wear?' asked Selina. 'I didn't bring anything with me.'

'That's all right,' said Oliver, opening one of the wall-to-wall wardrobe's many doors. 'I've had a dress sent here for you. It should be… yes, here it is.' He removed it from the rail and held it up. 'What do you think?'

He saw Selina looking appreciatively at the dress and realised that she couldn't imagine exactly how it would look on her. All the underwear you'll need is in the top drawer,' he added, pointing to an ornate dresser. 'You won't need panties; I want you naked between your thighs so anyone can touch you whenever they like.'

Savouring the stricken expression on her face he turned away, leaving her to prepare herself for the coming evening.

Selina stood beside Oliver in the hallway of his townhouse, nervously awaiting the arrival of their dinner guests. Her dress had a mauve corseted bodice and a full lilac and white skirt that fell in soft folds to just below the knee. The bodice fitted very tightly, and when she leant forward a fraction it was just possible to see the tops of her nipples. Despite the fact that she knew no one else was aware of it she felt horribly naked without panties, and as she stood there her fingers plucked agitatedly at her skirt.

'Stop fidgeting,' snapped Oliver as the doorbell rang and the butler showed in four of the six guests. There was a flurry of introductions and Selina, despite Oliver's orders to look every guest directly in the eye when she met them, found herself glancing shyly away and only formed a fleeting impression of each of them.

Harry, the banker, was of average build and appearance, but his wife, Charlotte, was a statuesque blonde wearing a sugar-pink semi-transparent outfit of trousers and hip-length jacket and camisole top.

Christian Wells, the man whom Kim had told her about, was shorter than Oliver, and slimmer. He stood very straight and had short brown hair and rather gentle brown eyes. He looked more like Selina imagined barristers would look, and seemed at first glance to be a less dominating and charismatic personality than Oliver. He was accompanied by a girl named Jilly. She was also slender, of average height, with curly brown hair and brown eyes that were surprisingly similar to Christian's. It didn't appear that in their case opposites attracted, thought Selina.

'Georgina warned me she might be late,' said Oliver, leading his guests through into the small ante-room where a tray of drinks had been prepared. 'Help yourselves to whatever you want,' he added, waving his hand towards the sherry, champagne, and bucks fizz.

'I understand from your office that you've been taking some holiday,' said Christian to Oliver. His voice was quiet, almost caressing, which Selina found very attractive.

'All work and no play makes Oliver a dull boy,' the host reasoned.

'And when did you find that out?' asked Christian. 'This must be the first holiday you've taken in more than a year.'

'I had some training to do,' explained Oliver, sliding his hand beneath Selina's long hair and idly caressing the nape of her neck. 'We've been busy, haven't we, Selina?'

Selina realised they were all staring at her, staring with

hungry, predatory eyes, and her stomach tightened with fear. 'Yes, we have,' she murmured in confirmation.

'How exciting,' said Christian. 'And this is her introduction to London society, is it Oliver?'

'Indeed it is. It's a little sooner than I'd intended,' he turned to the banker, 'but I understand you're going away on business, Harry, and this was the only date you could make.'

Harry looked surprised. 'Not exactly, old chap. I'm away next month. You must have misunderstood what Georgina told you.'

'I doubt that,' said Oliver.

'How very curious,' said Christian. 'It's not like Georgina to get things wrong.' He smiled charmingly at the lovely young hostess. 'Did you know she's one of the most successful lawyers in London, Selina?'

'I – I don't know very much about Georgina,' the girl explained. 'In fact, I don't know very much about Oliver's work either.'

'And do you come to London very often?' asked Christian, with clearly growing interest.

'I've never been before,' she confessed.

'Then we must make sure your first visit is a memorable one.'

'Hear, hear,' agreed Harry, draining his glass and instantly picking up another full one.

Feeling more and more nervous with every passing minute, Selina did the same, but Oliver caught hold of her wrist.

'I don't want you drinking too much tonight,' he said quietly, taking the full glass from her, 'it'll dull your responses. One more glass of wine with your dinner will be quite sufficient.'

Selina flushed as the others continued to stare at her.

Just as the silence was becoming oppressive there was a ring at the door, the butler again appeared from nowhere to open it, and Georgina waltzed in wearing a striking beige evening dress, ankle length but slit to the thigh, with a V-shaped back. From her left shoulder to below her right hip black flowers were printed across the fabric, while around her neck and hanging carelessly down her back was a long flowing black chiffon scarf.

'Not too late for a drink, I hope?' she asked flightily.

'Of course not, everyone else has only just arrived,' Oliver assured her. 'Do introduce us to your friend.'

It was only then that Selina dragged her eyes from the flamboyant woman and turned her attention to the petit girl standing quietly just behind Georgina. She looked about eighteen or nineteen, and similar in appearance to Kim, except that her shimmering black hair was waist-length and her face more heart-shaped. 'This is my Thai girl. Her name's Kara,' Georgina announced proudly. 'Isn't she just *divine*?'

Everyone's attention switched to Kara and Selina was shocked to note, through the girl's see-through white chiffon blouse, that her nipples had been pierced and silver nipple rings were outlined by the fabric. From the waist down she was covered by a turquoise sarong-style skirt, and had very high heels on her tiny feet, while pink nail varnish gleamed prettily on each of her toenails.

'Delighted to meet you Kara,' said Oliver, handing the girl a drink. But Georgina waved it away.

'I don't want Kara drinking tonight,' she said abruptly.

'Someone else who needs to be fully alert. This gets more exciting with every minute that passes,' remarked Christian, and Jilly, who hadn't uttered a word since the introductions, smiled fondly at him.

A few minutes later they all went through to dinner.

'Eat sparingly,' Oliver whispered in Selina's ear. 'Just the soup and a little dessert. Leave most of the main course. I don't want you feeling over-full and sleepy.'

During the first course all the talk around the table seemed to be of legal matters, and Selina stopped trying to follow it, concentrating instead on the faces of the guests. Although busy chattering, there was hardly a moment when one or other of them wasn't turning to look at her, their eyes questioning, probing, and although they smiled when they realised she was looking at them, their smiles did not seem particularly kind.

During the main course Selina was daydreaming about nothing and obediently pushing the succulent lamb around her plate as Oliver had ordered, when she suddenly became aware that Christian was no longer sitting at the table. She frowned, wondering how he could have left the room without her noticing and then, to her horror, she felt hands caressing her silk stockings beneath the table, and then the hands were actually parting her legs! She couldn't quite believe what was happening.

From the opposite end of the table Oliver watched her with evident interest, she noticed resentfully, as though she were some kind of laboratory experiment. But then she suppressed a squeal and forgot Oliver as lips delicately nipped and kissed the exposed flesh above the lacy band of her hold-up stockings. Occasionally a tongue would swirl around in small circles, very gradually inching higher and higher until she was sure its owner – Christian – would be able to feel her increasing heat and detect her scent of arousal.

Everyone else at the table was still eating and the hubbub of conversation continued with a bizarre normality, although the faces were continually turning in her direction, and she knew they were waiting to see what happened.

She'd never been so humiliated in all her life and gazed beseechingly at Oliver, but he ignored the mute appeal in her eyes and started to talk to Charlotte, who was sitting to his left.

Now Christian grew bolder. His mouth moved higher, his fingers parted her rapidly swelling sex lips, and his tongue darted between them, running up and down the moist channel until she felt her belly start to cramp. As her clitoris swelled he drew it into his mouth, sucking very gently, far more gently than Oliver had ever done. At the same time his fingers were sliding as far beneath her as they could, caressing that sensitive area of flesh between her private rear entrance and her pussy.

It was all too much for Selina. Her breasts gently heaved as she breathed deeply. She knew her face and throat were flushed with arousal because now everybody was staring at her, watching with interest as they waited for her pleasure to come, and suddenly she spasmed as the delicious warmth flooded through her and her body arched in brief sharp ecstasy.

'That looked nice,' purred Jilly. 'Christian's awfully clever with his tongue – it's one of his specialities.'

Selina couldn't answer, and she couldn't bear to look at any of them. Instead she lowered her head and, with trembling hands struggling to hold her cutlery, pretended to be interested in her food.

When Christian resumed his place at the table and smiled at her she looked away, mortified both at what he'd done to her and at the fact that she'd been unable to control herself despite being at a table full of strangers.

'Almost as tasty as the lamb,' he announced. 'I can't wait for dessert,' and everybody laughed.

Everybody except Oliver, who merely stared at Selina with one eyebrow raised as much as to say, 'I told you so'.

After the plates had been cleared Selina and the other guests waited for the dessert. Eventually the butler returned bearing a small glass bowl of fruit salad. He placed it in front of Selina before withdrawing from the room.

'So what about the rest of us?' Georgina asked brashly.

'Our dessert's going to be something rather special,' explained Oliver. 'But Selina won't be able to eat when we do, so I thought she should enjoy hers first.'

'That sounds intriguing,' Harry enthused. 'Your dinner parties are always exciting, old chap.'

'I hope this one lives up to expectations,' said Oliver, looking hard at Selina.

She didn't dare think what might lie ahead. Instead she finished the fruit salad and then sat waiting, hands folded in her lap, for whatever might happen next.

'We're going into the billiard room,' Oliver announced, and suddenly she was caught up in the midst of them as, chattering and laughing, they swept her along through the house and into the aforementioned arena.

'Lie on the table, Selina,' Oliver ordered without warning.

She didn't dare stop to question him, but simply slipped off her shoes and then did as he commanded.

'Now pull the dress up around your waist,' he continued. This time she did hesitate, remembering she was naked beneath the skirt. 'I hope you're not going to disappoint me,' he said in a level tone, and a chill ran down her spine. She knew only too well what those words meant... they meant punishment.

Hastily she pulled at the hem, closing her eyes to try and blot out the shame of exposing herself to everyone gathered around the end of the table.

'Open your eyes,' said Oliver. 'I don't want our guests to think you're falling asleep.'

'I'm sure there's no chance of that,' chuckled Jilly.

As Selina watched anxiously, Oliver brought a large bowl of cherries to the table and placed them between Selina's outspread legs. He pressed her feet flat to the green baize so that her knees were raised, and then pushed her thighs apart until she knew everyone must be able to see her sex, still puffy from where Christian had aroused her.

'We're having cherries in a yoghurt whip for dessert,' announced Oliver. 'The yoghurt whip is in a tube here. Which one of you ladies would like to put some of that inside Selina before the gentlemen fill her with the cherries?'

'Oh no!' cried Selina, automatically closing her thighs.

'Someone peel down the top of her dress,' ordered Oliver, and it was Georgina who was the first to move forward. She smiled down at the distraught girl and, as she lifted her a little and tugged at the zip and eased the bodice away from her full breasts, she flicked at each of the nipples in turn, making Selina jump.

'She's very sensitive here,' she informed the rest of the assembled guests. 'It's almost impossible for her not to come, if you pinch her nipples hard enough.'

'Later on I'll disprove that theory of yours,' said Oliver. 'She only comes when she's allowed to. Isn't that right, Selina?'

Selina could hardly speak, so intense was her humiliation. There was a sob in her voice as she tried to agree, but her obvious distress only seemed to excite the guests even more. She lay back and closed her eyes to the ordeal.

Suddenly someone, she thought it was Charlotte, was easing a plastic nozzle into the entrance of her vagina, and then she was being filled with a cool soft liquid. She jerked her hips away and the nozzle slipped out.

'Naughty, naughty,' said Harry reprovingly, and one of

his hands tightened round her right breast, the fingers digging cruelly into the flesh until she cried out with the discomfort of it. 'I'm sure you know better than to move when one of your master's guests is busy with you.'

Oliver tutted. 'A disappointment already.'

'Surely not,' said Christian swiftly. 'You hadn't warned her what was about to happen. It's an instinctive reaction, not one she could be expected to control.'

'I decide what she can and can't be expected to control,' said Oliver icily. 'She knows very well she's being disobedient, don't you Selina?'

Tears blurred her vision and meandered down her cheeks. If this was only the beginning of the evening, what on earth was going to happen to her by the end? 'I – I'm sorry,' she whispered, and then the nozzle was replaced and once more the liquid was squirted inside her... But suddenly it felt delicious and strangely exciting, and Selina's hips began to grind, despite her inbuilt reservations.

'I think she's getting into the swing of it now,' said Christian.

Harry's fingers, which had clearly been eager to inflict further punishment on her breasts, were withdrawn.

'Time for the cherries then,' said Oliver. 'I think you can see to those, Jilly. The men can wait. Please don't move while she's doing it, Selina. And you're not to come yet.'

Selina immediately tried to subdue the rising excitement she was experiencing, but Jilly clearly knew what she was doing. As she pushed cherry after cherry inside Selina her fingers swirled around the highly sensitive entrance until, with cruel deliberation, she held one of the cherries firmly against Selina's G-spot. She rolled it back and forth across the slightly raised segment of vaginal wall until Selina felt an ominous quaking begin in her abdomen, and her muscles felt as though they would tear with the effort as she bore down on them to prevent her orgasm. In doing so she forced out two of the cherries and some of the yoghurt, and without warning Oliver struck her a stinging blow with a latex whip right across her exposed nipples. She screamed in agony.

'I told you to keep still,' he reminded her coldly, and then he was trailing the latex around the soft undersides of her breasts in a movement that was almost a caress.

'I knew she wouldn't be able to resist that!' said Jilly gleefully, her busy fingers inserting more and more cherries until Selina began to panic.

'I can't take any more,' she cried. 'I'm so full it hurts,' and then she held her breath as a strong hand pressed down on the very lowest part of her belly. The most extraordinary sensations engulfed her as the stretched and tormented flesh quivered beneath the additional pressure.

'She does feel very full,' remarked Harry. 'I think that's probably enough. Can we start eating now, Oliver?'

Selina looked up at her master, and his eyes glinted avariciously as he continued to trail the whip over her engorged breasts, around the dark areolae that surrounded the rigid nipples, scarlet from the cruel lash of the whip.

'Of course,' he finally said. 'You must all be hungry. As for you Selina, you can come as often as you like now. Show us all how shamefully wanton you are.'

'Please don't,' she whimpered pitifully. But he'd already turned away, anxious for his share of the delicious dessert that would, she guessed, taste all the sweeter coming from her.

Immediately hands and lips were devouring her, tongues searching deeply, mouths sucking at the entrance to her moist yoghurt-filled channel, and she was nothing but a mass of sensations. Soon, every time a tongue swirled inside her or a cherry popped out of her frantic pussy, she was engulfed by a climax so that when they'd eventually finished she'd lost count of the number of times she'd come. She lay completely spent on the billiard table, breathing rapidly, unable to believe what they'd done to her and how she'd reacted.

Oliver pulled her off the table and faced her for a moment. 'Only one disappointment so far; that's very good,' he whispered. 'Let's see if you fare as well in the swimming pool.'

'The swimming pool!' exclaimed Jilly like an excited child. 'How wonderful!' And as Selina, still dazed by what had just happened, was led through into the pool area, she saw that Kara was already there, utterly naked between Georgina and Harry. They were each pulling on her nipple rings so that the poor buds were cruelly extended and her tiny breasts were pulled away from her ribs. The girl was whimpering, but despite that, Selina knew she was excited.

The swimming pool had been added on to the back of Oliver's house and was covered with a sliding glass roof, closed now that it was evening. Inside it was very warm. Within seconds everyone was stripping off their clothing, laying it on small benches pushed against the tiled walls. The men were visibly aroused by what had been happening to Selina on the billiard table, and she noticed in particular that Harry's cock was exceptionally thick, although not as long as Oliver's, and very red and angry-looking.

As Harry's eyes crept over the now naked Selina she felt her flesh crawl and started to step away from him, but immediately Oliver was behind her, one hand in the small of her back so that escape was impossible.

'If he wants you, he can have you,' he whispered in her ear, and she cringed against him, not daring to complain, but hoping against hope that Harry didn't want her.

After a few seconds, much to Selina's relief, Harry turned

his attention to Kara, and she could tell by the hungry look in his eye that he was more attracted to the slight Thai girl than to her.

'All right if I have a little fun with her?' she heard him courteously ask Georgina.

The voluptuous woman smiled. 'Of course it is. That's why I brought her. She loves company.'

Harry's pale blue eyes glittered with excitement. He pulled one of the benches away from the wall and bent the Thai's unresisting body over it. Then, without any preliminaries, he parted the tight buttocks and suddenly thrust his thick erection into the unprepared girl's rectum. Her scream of agonised protest rang around the swimming pool, and Selina glanced at Oliver in despair.

'He's hurting her badly,' she whispered.

'What's that to you?' asked Oliver. 'Just be grateful it was her he chose.'

Selina *was* grateful, but then she found herself being led round to the front of the Thai girl, and Oliver pushed her to her knees.

'Pull on her nipple rings,' he commanded. 'I consider them a rather good idea. Perhaps they'd suit you.'

Selina shivered. She could imagine only too well how much pain it must cause when the tender flesh of the nipples was pierced by cruel metal rings, but again she offered no protest because already she'd disobeyed Oliver once, and was terrified of disobeying again. She reached out and pulled tentatively on the gleaming metal. She watched the lovely Thai's face contort further as Harry continued to stab into her from behind, holding her hips, and now the discomfort he was clearly causing her was joined by pain from the nipples that Selina was manipulating so relentlessly.

'Get him to stop... please get him to stop,' Kara

whispered desperately, her voice so low that even Selina had difficulty in hearing her. 'It… it's too much… even for me.'

'What did she say?' Georgina suddenly demanded.

'I don't know,' lied Selina. 'I didn't understand.'

'Talking in her own language again, is she?' Georgina assumed incorrectly. 'You'll be punished for that later, Kara.' But Selina felt even that was preferable to Georgina knowing the truth.

As the Thai girl started to weep Selina withdrew her hands, and it was only when Oliver grasped her hair and spitefully tugged her head back that she resumed playing with the bizarre nipple decorations. This time she also squeezed the dark pink buds; squeezed them in the way she knew she liked, and she could tell that this new but more pleasurable pain was distracting the distraught Kara from what Harry was doing to her.

Harry increased his tempo, and every time he thrust into the girl, ramming home between the cheeks of her bottom, he started to slap the round globes of flesh with stinging blows, and at last seemed to trigger Kara's pleasure. Selina watched the girl's mouth twist in a mixture of agony and ecstasy as her tormented body began its ascent towards orgasm.

Suddenly, for reasons she didn't understand, Selina wanted to be the one who triggered the girl's release, and as Harry began to gasp and groan she drew one of the nipples into her mouth and closed her teeth around its base. She nipped sharply, while at the same time her tongue twirled the nipple ring. As she bit so Kara screamed, and then her body was twisting and turning and her avid reaction drew everyone nearer. They all stood and watched as Harry finally spilled himself into the contorted Thai, and Kara continued to groan with delight as Harry spanked her remorselessly, despite the fact that his own orgasm was over.

Eventually, when only Kara's sobbing could be heard, Georgina tapped Harry lightly on the shoulder. 'Better leave her alone now,' she suggested. 'You don't want to wear her out before the evening's over.'

'I don't want him to wear himself out,' said Charlotte, brushing her long blonde hair back off her shoulders. Harry smiled at her, sliding an arm around her naked waist, his fingers digging into the soft flesh.

'Turn you on, did it?' he asked.

'See for yourself,' invited Charlotte, parting her legs, and immediately Harry fell to his knees and began tonguing between her thighs, lapping eagerly at the juices that Selina could see covering the girl's fine blonde pubic hair.

'And what about Selina?' Christian quietly asked. 'We don't want her to feel left out. After all, it's her first dinner party, and she is the hostess.'

'And what did you have in mind?' asked Oliver.

'Something in the pool, I think,' said Christian, and he turned and dived athletically into the clear blue water. Surfacing with a laugh he ran his fingers through his wet hair and blinked the water out of his eyes. 'Come and join me, Selina,' he called.

Selina's knees began to buckle and she looked at Oliver in wide-eyed terror. 'I... I can't swim,' she stammered.

'It's a little late to tell me now,' he remarked scornfully, and before she knew what was happening he'd picked her up and thrown her to Christian.

It was without doubt the worst moment of Selina's life. Nothing that had gone before, however humiliating, had filled her with a similar terror, and the instant she sploshed into the water she sank like a stone. Christian was quickly under the surface next to her, his arms around her waist as he pulled her up, and at last her head broke the surface and she gulped in great mouthfuls of air, coughing and spluttering.

'It seems you'll have to rely on the rest of us to keep you afloat,' Christian said thoughtfully, and when she looked at him his eyes, unlike Oliver's, were quite kind. 'Throw in one of those rings,' he called to Jilly, and then Selina was manhandled onto the blue circular tube that his girlfriend had tossed him.

It was clear that Selina fascinated Christian. She watched as he floated around her, treading water. Occasionally he reached beneath the rubber ring and toyed idly with her vulva, before scooping up some water in his palms and then letting it trickle down between her breasts. Some of it filled her navel and he leant across her, flicking it out with a finger in a surprisingly erotic caress. Selina wriggled within the confines of the ring.

Oliver and Jilly joined them in the water, while Harry, Charlotte and Georgina took the unsteady Kara into the spa bath. Almost immediately Selina heard the Thai girl crying out as they began to amuse themselves with her in the bubbling water.

Oliver swam slowly up and down the pool, occasionally pausing to watch Christian's careless manipulations of Selina's body, but she could tell nothing from the expression on his face. Jilly spent a lot of time caressing Selina's highly sensitive breasts, but to Selina's disappointment she ignored the nipples, concentrating instead on the beautifully rounded breasts themselves. She drew circles around them with her fingers, squeezed them lightly, and pressed them together before running the tip of her tongue across the wet surface.

It was all very gentle and arousing. For the first time since Oliver had taken over as master at Summerfield Hall, Selina began to relax as softly pleasurable sensations radiated through her body. Twice she orgasmed as Christian and Jilly worked on her, but they were a different kind of orgasm from the ones Oliver had taught her; far quieter and calmer. She relaxed and felt her eyelids begin to droop.

That was a mistake.

The moment she closed her eyes Christian thrust three fingers inside her, moving them roughly around, and she gasped with the unexpected and uninvited invasion. As he worked he put a hand beneath her buttocks, raising her up a little and then, just as his fingers ignited the first sparks of pleasurable pain, he lowered his head and sunk his teeth into the soft flesh of her belly. This time she cried out in pain, and suddenly the terrible dark pleasure was engulfing her again and her muscles contracted into harsh rhythmic pulses as her pleasure spilled over once more.

'He's certainly taught you to like pain,' hissed Christian, withdrawing his fingers and sadistically tipping her out of the tyre. Selina screamed and gurgled once more, terrified as the water closed over her head, but this time it was Oliver who dragged her up and towed her towards the shallow end of the pool, where she was able to stand with the water just reaching her armpits.

'Did you come then?' he asked casually.

'Y-yes,' coughed Selina, fighting for breath, her goose-pimpled breasts heaving invitingly.

'Does he turn you on?' Oliver persisted, watching her closely.

Selina fought to calm herself, and her breathing gradually slowed. She stared at the grinning Christian, her opinion of him rapidly changing. 'It… it wasn't him,' she managed. 'It was what he did to me.'

Oliver nodded.

'I think I'd like some pleasure now,' said Christian, swimming up to join them. He settled himself in the corner of the shallow end of the pool with his arms resting on the sides and his legs floating on the water in front of him. His long narrow cock bobbed up through the lapping surface. 'I want her to suck me off,' he said to Oliver, and Selina's heart sank as quickly as she had as she felt him pushing her towards where Christian was waiting.

'Just a straight blow-job?' he asked his rival and guest.

'Oh, that's a bit boring,' smiled Christian, with annoying arrogance. 'Let's set a time limit on it. Say, two minutes to make me come, and if she fails it's another punishment on the old scoreboard.'

'Sounds okay to me,' agreed Oliver.

'I think she should only be allowed to use her mouth,' offered Jilly, who had floated up beside Selina. 'Give me something so I can tie her hands behind her back.'

Oliver eased himself effortlessly out of the water and retrieved the belt from his discarded trousers. He threw it to Jilly, who pulled the helpless Selina's arms behind her back and buckled her wrists tightly together. Selina winced as the leather bit into her flesh.

'He's got *incredible* self-control,' Jilly taunted Selina. 'You'll have to be *extremely* skilful to make him come inside two minutes.'

'Time to begin,' called Oliver, checking the clock on the wall.

Selina knew she had little option but to comply. She waded closer, between the grinning man's thighs, took a deep breath, and bent to accept his bobbing helmet into her mouth. Her tongue lapped around the swollen glans in the way she'd been taught back at Summerfield Hall. She thought it would be easy, because he was so clearly excited by all that had gone on, but quickly realised she'd seriously underestimated his will power. Despite her concerted efforts to please him with her tongue and lips he merely floated

127

there, goading her with his eyes. It was as though she was having no effect on him at all.

It was then that Selina realised how devious it had been to prevent her from using her hands. If she'd been able to add the stimulation of her fingers, she was certain he'd have spilt his seed almost immediately, but her relatively inexperienced mouth alone didn't seem effective enough.

'Only ten seconds to go,' called Oliver, and despairingly Selina redoubled her efforts. But although Christian's hips jerked in the water, she knew he wasn't going to come until he was absolutely ready – and she knew that wouldn't be within the two minutes.

'Time up,' called Oliver, and the moment he'd spoken Selina felt the stalk stretching her lips throb, and then with a groan Christian was coming – coming as though he was never going to stop. Selina swallowed as fast as she could, but she started to choke and panic, attempting to withdraw, only Jilly wouldn't let her. She held Selina until the poor girl had consumed every last drop of his seed.

'Another disappointment,' said Oliver harshly, and Selina lifted her head to look up at him, hoping to see some sign of understanding on his face. But there was none.

'That's twice you've let me down tonight,' he reminded her.

'When's she going to be punished?' asked Christian, dreamily.

'When you all come to Summerfield Hall next weekend,' replied Oliver. 'If you arrive after lunch the punishment will be administered during the afternoon, before the dinner in the evening.'

'That should be interesting,' remarked Christian, and Selina sensed that the apparent kindness in his eyes was dangerously deceptive. At that moment, he didn't seem very different from Oliver.

'I think I'd like to borrow Jilly,' said Oliver, throwing something into the pool next to Christian. 'Why don't you have some fun with this and Selina while we're busy.'

Christian grasped the toy he'd been thrown and nodded. 'Go ahead. Jilly won't mind, will you my dear?'

Jilly smiled and climbed out of the pool. Selina knew without being told that Oliver wasn't going to hurt Jilly. He was probably going to make love to her properly, giving the pleasure without the pain, and she wondered why it was that he so rarely allowed her to have her pleasure that way.

'What are you thinking?' asked Christian with interest, the water surging around him as he stood upright.

'Nothing,' replied Selina.

Christian gripped one of her breasts tightly and squeezed hard. 'Don't lie to me. You were thinking about something… tell me what, or I'll report you to Oliver.'

'I – I was just wondering why he takes such pleasure in hurting me,' she confessed timidly.

Christian studied her closely. 'You're not jealous of him and Jilly, I hope? You're special, Selina. You must be, or Oliver wouldn't waste his time on you. As for hurting you… well, you enjoy it, don't you?'

'But it's wrong,' she protested. 'That's not what lovemaking's meant to be about.'

'I think you're getting things confused,' remarked Christian. 'Oliver isn't really into lovemaking, he's into sex. That's not the same thing at all. Besides, you wouldn't be satisfied with ordinary sex, especially now.' He chuckled to himself. 'Not that you'll necessarily want to go as far as he does, of course. It's always interesting for the rest of us to see at what point his girls fall by the wayside. I'm particularly interested in you, Selina, because you fascinate me. There's something very different about you.'

'W-what did he throw into the pool?' she stammered, feeling uncomfortable with his sudden intensity and wanting to change the subject.

'You'll find out in a minute,' he replied, his eyes never leaving her. 'Now, I want you to get into the corner of the pool where I was a few minutes ago, and float your legs out just as I did. I'll just take the belt off your wrists and put a couple of floats round your ankles, as you're a non-swimmer.'

Selina's hands were swiftly freed and then she was wedged in the corner, her arms resting against the cool tiles at the side. The floats were fastened around her ankles, and she blushed as her legs rose to the surface.

Christian waded between them, pushed her thighs apart, and lifted her lower torso a little, but all the time he kept one hand beneath the water and Selina couldn't see what was in it.

'Close your eyes,' he instructed, and she warily obeyed.

There was a long pause, and then without any warning, she suddenly felt her vagina and her rectum being invaded as Christian thrust a double vibrator inside her.

'It's waterproof,' he assured her with glee. 'You should find it very exciting.'

'But it's hurting me,' she protested, squirming against the obscene double invasion. She tried to complain again, but the two plastic intruders suddenly began to vibrate and took her voice away.

The two contrasting movements were incredible, and immediately her pleasure started to simmer. It felt as though the relentlessly probing, vibrating plastic toy was going to tear her apart as her muscles cramped frantically. Inside her tummy it felt as though a balloon was inflating, swelling rapidly until, as the probe inside her rectum rubbed against the sensitive inner walls, the balloon seemed to burst and flood her with a warm soothing liquid.

Her back arched up from the water, and as the climax continued to tear through her Christian slapped her belly slowly and steadily with the backs of the fingers of both hands.

This only intensified Selina's pleasure, and she could hear herself screaming with ecstasy, because although her climax had subsided the probes continued their ceaseless work and rekindled her raging desires.

'You're wonderfully depraved,' Christian enthused. 'I wish you could see the expression on your face now.'

Selina felt herself flushing with shame, but there was nothing she could do because Oliver had already trained her body to desire – no, more than that – to need this painful excitement in order to gain true release.

Christian's hands had now left her belly and were slapping her breasts, the fingers flicking with deadly accuracy at the points of her incredibly swollen nipples, and yet again a stunning climax ripped through her.

'One more for luck,' said Christian, when the last few contractions had died away.

'No more,' begged Selina.

'But I like to see you come,' he explained, his tone almost kindly. But Selina knew he wasn't kind; he was very much like Oliver, and he was enjoying her helpless torment.

'Please, take them out,' she implored.

'How prettily you beg,' he taunted, and then the probes began moving again. This time Christian increased the speed so that her tortured nerve-endings sent flashing messages of pain to her foggy brain, and she started to thrash around in the water, attempting to dislodge the vile intruders. But Christian's hands firmly restrained her.

Now she was forced to endure yet another shattering climax. She groaned with despair at the heavy pressure building behind her clitoris, and when it finally exploded and her body went rigid she felt as though she was going to faint with the intensity of the feelings.

Eventually, when her body was still, Christian took pity on her and removed the twin vibrator, but he couldn't resist cupping her vulva with his hand and pressing hard against the tormented flesh. To her everlasting shame Selina felt herself pressing down against him, enjoying the dreadful sensation of exhausted flesh being stimulated against its will, and with a smile Christian pressed harder against her crotch, moving the heel of his hand. As her clitoris was indirectly stimulated Selina was forced to endure one final dark explosion before, sobbing at her own depravity, she was released and allowed to crawl up the steps and out of the pool.

Oliver was waiting, and handed a towelling robe to her.

'Dry yourself,' he said. 'The evening's nearly over.'

Selina glanced beyond him to where Jilly was standing. The slim brunette had a look of intense satisfaction on her face, and a contented smile played around her lips. Selina was shocked as a sharp pang of jealousy stabbed into her soul. She cringed at the thought of that woman touching her Oliver. She felt betrayed, as though he'd done something unforgivable, but she knew she had no right to feel that way. Oliver was free, whereas she was not, and the realisation made her want to cry.

Everybody dried themselves and dressed, and then returned to the drawing room, where Selina felt ridiculously out of place in the towelling robe.

'You're the guest of honour tonight, Harry,' said Oliver. 'Before the evening concludes, is there anything in particular you'd like to do or see?'

Harry nodded enthusiastically. 'Yes,' he admitted, 'there is one thing.'

Oliver raised his eyebrows, and Harry looked across at Selina. 'I'd like to see her and Kara bringing each other off,' he said excitedly. 'Perhaps you could turn it into some sort of a contest?'

'Certainly,' agreed Oliver, casually.

Selina looked despairingly at the Thai girl, who hastily lowered her own eyes, clearly trying to hide the expression in them.

'I tell you what we'll do...' Oliver was still talking, '...We'll take them upstairs, put them on a bed together, and they can take it in turns to make each other come. The one who resists her orgasm the longest is the winner...' he grinned evilly, '...and the loser gets punished. If it's Selina I'll choose the punishment and add it on next weekend. And if it's Kara who loses, Georgina can choose her punishment.'

'I don't think Kara will lose,' boasted Georgina.

Selina didn't think so either. Harry, either by accident or through sheer cruelty, was going to make her disappoint Oliver yet again, but even as she and Kara were pushed and jostled up the stairs, Selina realised that her exhausted flesh was beginning to prickle with excitement at the prospect of what was to come.

Chapter Eight

Selina stared anxiously at the king-size bed that dominated the large room, and then put up a token and easily quashed resistance as Oliver slipped the towelling robe from her shoulders and then eased her back onto the luxuriously soft mattress. He turned to Harry and raised an enquiring eyebrow.

'I want to see Kara working on this gorgeous girl of yours first,' said Harry, in response to the unspoken question.

A tiny smile of approval danced across Oliver's lips as he slid a soft pillow from the head of the bed and pushed it beneath Selina's bottom, raising her hips. Without looking, he knew Christian was more than anxious to get his hands on her to orchestrate the preparations, and felt immense satisfaction that his arch rival was taking such an interest in his delicious property. He revelled in Christian's envy, both professionally and sexually. The episode in the pool was only to heighten his rival's interest, deliberately calculated to intensify his disappointment when Selina was ultimately denied him.

Oliver moved to the foot of the bed and his guests gathered around as the Thai girl stripped and then gracefully climbed astride Selina's hips. She bent forward and started to gently massage the breasts thrust so temptingly up before her. Her tiny hands moved deftly over the pale flesh, squeezing and stroking each globe in turn.

Kara continued to massage Selina's breasts as the minutes slowly ticked by on the clock beside the bed. Then the sensual girl moved lower and began to massage Selina's abdomen, her thumbs pressing into her flat stomach, her delicately strong fingers spread, expertly stroking and probing the soft tissue. And when Selina responded with a slight gasp Kara immediately shifted lower and inserted a finger into the tormented girl's slippery opening.

Oliver watched as Selina's hips began to undulate under the deft movements of the finger, and barely audible moans of delight drifted from her slightly parted lips. Clearly she was desperate to come, but was bravely denying herself for as long as possible. Oliver gazed down at her rosy face and the enchanting determination etched there, and felt his penis thicken at the mouthwatering sight. Selina's fingers clawed at the satin sheets, and her back arched as Kara increased her endeavors and buried her face between her victim's taut thighs.

She licked like a cat with the cream, and Selina's moans increased and her body writhed helplessly as she pushed up from the pillow, beyond resisting now and straining for the ultimate touch that would detonate her orgasm.

Fingers pinched her nipples, and then the clever Thai slipped between Selina's thighs, opened her succulent sex lips, and squashed one of her breasts between them. The audience watched in silent awe as the erect nipple contacted Selina's equally erect clitoris, and then she shuddered, fed the satin sheet between her tightly clenched teeth, and thrashed her head insanely from side to side as she climaxed.

There was a long silence as the audience absorbed the eroticism of what they had just been privileged to witness. The spell was only broken when someone quietly coughed.

Oliver stirred himself and turned to Georgina. 'How long did Selina manage to resist?' he asked, his voice almost betraying his lust.

'Um,' Georgina, too, was uncharacteristically flustered

as she tore her eyes from the beautifully entwined bodies on the rumpled sheets and checked the clock. 'Just over six minutes,' she declared.

'Okay. We'll give her a few minutes to recover, and then we'll see how Kara can do.' Even as he spoke, Oliver knew it was no contest. He had no doubt that the Thai would have far more resolve than his girl. But he wasn't sorry about the impending defeat to Georgina, for it would merely mean another delicious punishment to be administered to Selina during the following weekend.

After the brief respite proceedings recommenced, and Selina made Kara lie on her stomach over the pillow. She pushed the dusky girl's thighs apart and teased her wet sex, parting the lips and drawing her fingers up and down against the already erect clitoris that nestled there. She worked diligently, her brow creased in concentration, her fingers squelching as they moved in earnest. But the minutes ticked by and, although clearly acutely aroused, Kara remained comfortably in control. Selina increased her efforts as the clock ticked relentlessly to the six minute mark, but then it passed and she knew she was beaten. At that moment Kara ground her sex down onto the busy fingers and allowed herself the luxury of a gentle, almost patronising orgasm.

'It wasn't even a contest,' the victorious Georgina gloated. 'Never mind Selina, no doubt you'll do better when you've had more training,' she added condescendingly.

'It would appear that there's still some significant work to be done,' Oliver conceded, before addressing his assembled guests. 'That's it for tonight everyone. I trust you've all had an enjoyable time.'

'Wonderful,' Harry enthused. 'That really rounded the evening off perfectly. I look forward to seeing Selina next weekend at Summerfield Hall.'

'Ditto,' said Christian. 'And we'll all get a turn at being intimate with Selina,' he presumed, rather than asked. 'And that's something I'm allowed to look forward to, I'm sure.' Oliver knew he was being challenged. 'And hopefully something Selina will look forward to as well,' Christian added. As the exhausted girl rose and slipped into her robe he reached out and tenderly stroked her hot cheek. Oliver saw her eyes widen, and there was something in her expression; a look of pleasure, but a look that was different from when he touched her. Oliver stared at Christian coldly.

Once the guests had departed he dragged Selina up to the tiny attic bedroom. He was angered by Christian's arrogance, and so Selina had to pay.

He pushed her down onto the rickety metal cot and tied her wrists and ankles to the frame.

'I'll come and release you at about seven,' he said curtly. 'We'll be driving straight back to Lincolnshire.'

'What have I done wrong?' she pleaded.

'You've disappointed me, Selina.' And without another word of explanation he switched off the light and locked the door.

Back in his room he slumped onto the huge bed. He could smell Selina on the satin sheets, and was startled by the intensity of feeling that that brief glance of attraction between she and Christian had caused in him.

Selina slept for most of the journey home to Lincolnshire. Her head was still full of the extraordinary events of the previous night, and even in her restless dreams Harry, Christian, Charlotte, Jilly, Georgina and Kara were there, their hands and mouths bringing her to peaks of ecstasy as they danced a strange erotic dance, continually changing partners.

When she awoke Oliver was just pulling into the

driveway of Summerfield Hall, and he turned to her.

'Didn't you sleep well last night?' he enquired.

'Not particularly,' she said bluntly, remembering how uncomfortable being tied to the cot had been.

'What did you think of my guests?'

She pondered for a moment. 'They were... interesting.'

Oliver chuckled. 'What a tactful answer! And who did you like the most?'

Selina didn't particularly *like* any of them, but she *disliked* Christian less than the others. However, she knew better than to say as much. 'I didn't really get to know any of them well enough to choose,' she hedged.

'Oh, I thought you got to know them very well indeed,' he said dryly.

'I wasn't talking about sexually.'

'I was,' he retorted. 'And I think you did have a favourite.'

'Then you know more than I do,' Selina said daringly, but he didn't respond.

For the rest of that day Selina was left alone to make sure everything was running smoothly in the house, and that Mrs Soames wasn't having any problems.

That evening she ate with Jake and Mary. Mrs Soames served Oliver his meal, and by the time Selina went to bed that night she felt somewhat confused.

During the previous evening she'd been paraded as Oliver's mistress and new plaything before his friends and associates. But a mere twenty-four hours later she was being treated like a skivvy, banished to the kitchen, and she didn't like it. It wasn't so much the changes in social position that distressed her, as the sudden cessation of attention and sexual stimulation. She realised that because Oliver had tutored her so relentlessly her body now expected to be continually aroused and satisfied, and when

138

it wasn't she felt irritable and out-of-sorts.

She was beginning to need the pain-filled pleasure, the incredible eroticism that Oliver had taught her, much as a drug addict would need a fix. She wondered what would happen if Oliver should tire of her, as he'd clearly tired of all his previous girls. She didn't want to be discarded by him. Who else could provide her with the pleasures she now needed?

Chapter Nine

In the morning Mary shook Selina awake, and as she yawned and stretched she looked at the auburn maid in surprise. 'What's the time?' she asked sleepily. 'My alarm hasn't gone off yet.'

'It's only six-forty-five, but I've been sent to dress you.'

Selina felt a slow stirring of excitement. Without protest she swung her legs out of the bed. As she peeled off her nightshirt she knew that the other girl was watching her closely, her strange green eyes alert and missing nothing. 'So what am I to wear today?' she asked.

'It's all in here,' explained Mary, putting a small leather case on Selina's bed. Opening it Selina pulled out an extraordinary collection of leather straps and rings, each connected to the other. 'What is all this?' she asked.

'Haven't you worn one before?' asked Mary, incredulously. 'It's a body harness. Here, I'll help you put it on.'

Her hands moved swiftly, easing Selina's breasts into the metal hoops that were harnessed by a network of body straps. Then Selina sat on the bed so Mary could feed her legs through the lower part of the harness. Next she eased the leather crotch-strap up between Selina's thighs until the bewildered girl felt it pressing against her sex lips.

'Very nice,' murmured Mary as she worked. 'Only one thing more and you're ready.'

Selina glanced into the suitcase and saw a leather studded collar lying there. Mary fastened it around her neck, pulling it almost uncomfortably tight and then, without another word but with a furtive glance of interest, she surprised her trussed mistress by leaving the room.

Slowly Selina walked over to the mirror and looked at her reflection. There was no denying the eroticism of the outfit. Her breasts were lifted high by the undersides of the hoops and jutted proudly forward, while the tightness of the leather crotch and the attached straps provided an insistent stimulus that was already causing her pulse to quicken.

She was still studying herself when her door opened and Oliver entered. 'I see Mary carried out my orders,' he remarked.

Selina felt suddenly shy, unable to turn and face him. She heard his footsteps on the carpet, and then he was standing behind her, staring into her reflection so that their eyes met in the mirror. She shivered slightly as he reached round in front of her and pinched the tender flesh of her breasts as the nipples swelled and throbbed, desperate to feel his touch.

'Such greedy little nipples,' he murmured.

Selina moaned softly, wishing she could move, to force him to touch her where she wanted to be touched, but she knew that that would be construed as disobedience and even more punishments would await her.

'I know what you'd like now,' he said huskily. The pinching intensified, and Selina started to squirm as the forbidden pleasure mounted, and through his trousers she could feel his erection brushing against her buttocks as she continued to writhe with rising excitement. Just as the pain was about to topple over into climax-inducing pleasure he released her nipples, leaving them scarlet and swollen. 'Later,' he muttered, but whether to her or to himself, Selina didn't know.

'Apart from your outfit this is a perfectly normal day,'

Oliver explained, as he resumed an air of normality and moved towards the door. 'You must carry out all the duties you would normally carry out, and no one is to touch you except for me. Do you understand?'

Selina understood only too well. She was in for another day of humiliation and frustration – frustration that only Oliver could relieve, and despite her best intentions a whimper of protest escaped from her throat.

'What's the matter?' he asked with deceptive kindness.

'Nothing,' she said hastily.

'Good.'

And then he was gone.

After a couple of hours Selina realised with surprise that she was hardly aware of what she was wearing. It almost seemed natural to be walking round Summerfield Hall dressed in such strange bondage garments, and she held her head high as she walked from room to room, even relishing the hard pressure of the leather between her thighs when she bent or knelt to do household tasks.

It was at lunchtime that disaster struck.

During the morning she'd been vaguely aware that Jake had been around more than usual, and whenever he passed he stared intently at her. Knowing that he'd worked for Oliver for so long she had been surprised because she couldn't believe that this was the first time he'd seen someone walking around one of Oliver's houses in a body harness. However, when she was sitting alone in the kitchen eating her lunch Jake came in from the garden and sat down at the table with her. This was the first time she'd seen him in the kitchen during the day and she felt vaguely uneasy, wishing that Mary was around.

'You can't imagine what you do to me when you're walking round like that,' he said suddenly. 'I can hardly keep my hands off you.'

Selina decided to ignore him, and when he stood up she pressed herself as far back as possible in her chair, remembering Oliver's words of warning.

'You want to be touched,' he continued. 'I can see it in your eyes, and you're already aroused.' As he said that he flicked contemptuously at one of her nipples, and the traitorous bud immediately stiffened. 'You fancy me too, don't you?' he persisted.

'You're not to touch me,' hissed Selina, terrified that either Mary or Oliver would walk in on the scene.

'No one will know,' he coaxed, standing behind her and brazenly cupping her breasts, his hungry fingers moulding the soft flesh until each globe grew heavy with wanting.

'Please leave me alone,' whimpered Selina. 'It's forbidden.'

'I can't,' said Jake roughly, and catching hold of her studded collar he pulled her up out of the chair, and then his hand was sliding down inside the leather between her thighs and when he drew his fingers out they were wet with her juices. 'Now tell me you don't fancy me,' he demanded.

'Just leave me alone,' she beseeched him, feeling her desire flaring but knowing she mustn't give in to it. 'I'll be punished, and so will you!'

'But no one will know,' he repeated urgently. He knelt down between her legs and one hand continued to massage between her thighs while his mouth moved hungrily from one breast to the other, sucking and biting. When he thrust two fingers inside her she felt the delicious warmth beginning, and suddenly her body was arching and spasming until eventually she slumped back against the chair, breathless and terrified.

'You – you shouldn't have done that.' Fear had dried

her throat and her voice croaked.

'But you loved it,' he panted, and then he was releasing his engorged member from his jeans, pulling her to her feet and sandwiching it against her belly. He was rubbing frantically, moving faster and faster, and without thinking Selina thrust her hips forward hoping he would penetrate her, but he shuddered and came before he could and she felt the hot liquid squirting up against the underside of her breasts and then spilling down over her stomach. With a cry of shame and secret frustration she tried to push him away.

'Jake!' cried Mary from the doorway, and Selina's eyes met the maid's in guilty horror. 'Get away from her Jake!' ordered Mary angrily. 'What were you thinking of?'

'I couldn't help it,' he blurted. 'She made me do it. She was desperate, said she couldn't go any longer without an orgasm. I was only doing what she demanded.'

'That's a lie!' protested Selina, unable to believe what she was hearing. 'He wouldn't let go of me. I told him it was wrong but he said no one would know!'

'But I know,' said Mary, her voice uncompromising.

'Please, don't tell Oliver,' Selina beseeched her.

'Why not?' she sneered. 'You should have thought about that before you persuaded Jake to pleasure you.'

'I didn't persuade him! He forced himself on me!'

'You could have called for help,' Mary smugly pointed out.

Selina didn't know what to say. It was true; she could have called for help. But it had all felt so delicious, and once again her wanton body had betrayed her. 'You won't tell, will you?' she meekly asked the auburn girl.

'Yes, I will,' Mary admitted bluntly. 'It's my duty. Oliver would expect me to tell him, and if I didn't he'd probably dismiss me.'

'But he'll punish me,' cried Selina, desperately wishing she could turn the clock back a few minutes.

'He'll probably punish Jake as well,' said Mary, with evident satisfaction. 'And you'll be to blame for that too.'

Selina couldn't bear it any more. Leaving the pair of them in the kitchen she hurried outside, drawing deep lungfuls of fresh air as she tried to calm her jangling nerves. Despite her trepidation she could still remember the excitement and the urgency she'd felt as Jake had brought himself off against her. She felt her clitoris swell and her hips began to move as she realised she could provide her own stimulation by using the leather that was digging so tightly into her vulva.

She was just teetering on the edge of an orgasm when, from the corner of her eye, she saw a shadowy figure standing at the study window looking out at her, and realised it was Oliver. Hastily she began to walk briskly across the garden, hoping she'd been too far away for him to realise what she'd been doing. Anyway, she thought to herself, she hadn't done anything wrong because she hadn't come, and no one else had been touching her.

Oliver remained shut away in his study for the rest of the day. Mrs Soames explained to Selina that he'd received a phone call from London and was working on the defence of a new client.

'It's unusual for him to take so much as a day off work, never mind two weeks,' the housekeeper said as she prepared the evening meal. 'You're very honoured.'

Selina wasn't sure that's how she would have described it, but she nodded and smiled, determined to at least keep Mrs Soames on her side.

'He asked that you serve him his dinner tonight,' the housekeeper continued.

'In this outfit?'

'Of course,' replied the older woman.

Selina studied her in silence for a few minutes. 'How long have you been with him?' she eventually asked, wondering if she could tell her some secrets about the enigmatic Oliver; give her some information that might help explain him to her.

'Five years, and I've signed a secrecy agreement,' said Mrs Soames abruptly, clearly guessing the girl's intent.

With a sigh Selina left the room; it was quite apparent that she wasn't going to get any information from that quarter.

The moment Selina entered the dining room carrying Oliver's first course that evening she felt an incredible air of eroticism in the room. His eyes surveyed her approvingly, his gaze almost a caress, and when she approached and placed the salmon mousse in front of him he slid a hand up the side of her leg and smiled at her.

'I saw you in the garden at lunchtime,' he remarked. 'You looked sensational. I don't think you have any idea just how much you excite me.'

Selina trembled at his words. His voice was gentle, his touch soft and sensual, but as always there was the latent threat of punishment. She waited tensely in case he'd noticed what she was trying to do to herself in the garden. But as his fingers trailed lazily over her exposed buttocks he gave no sign that there was anything wrong.

'You've done even better than I'd hoped,' he said. 'I had no idea how quickly you'd come to desire the pleasures that you've been taught. What a waste of all those years when you were locked away here.'

'I wasn't like this before I met you,' she reasoned, mesmerised by the touch of his fingers on her bare flesh. 'I know I've changed, but it's all because of you.'

146

'I'm only showing you what you're really like...'

Selina half turned to go, but was checked by the question she'd most dreaded.

'I trust no one touched you today?'

She hesitated, her face hidden from him. She wanted desperately to lie, to pretend that the incident in the kitchen had never happened, but if she lied and he knew then that was a double act of treachery – something she dared not risk.

'Well?' his voice was harsher now.

'Jake... Jake did...'

She closed her eyes and held her breath, waiting for his wrath.

'Turn and look at me,' he commanded.

Selina turned. She wished she could tell more from the expression on his face, but his eyes gave nothing away.

'*Who* touched you... and when?' he demanded slowly.

'Jake,' she confirmed, her voice no more than a timid whisper. 'In the kitchen.'

'At least you've more sense than to lie to me.' His unexpected response bemused the terrified girl, and she opened her eyes cautiously. 'I'll ring when I'm ready for my next course.'

Back in the kitchen Selina had to sit down because her legs felt so weak. Clearly he'd already known the answer before he'd asked the question, which meant that, true to her word, Mary had told him. Now she had to wait to see what her punishment would be.

'Anything wrong?' asked Mrs Soames as she busied herself with the main course.

'No,' lied Selina.

The housekeeper looked thoughtfully at her. 'You're not the first girl, you know,' she said. 'And you won't be the last. Why don't you just leave?'

'Leave?' Selina's voice rose in disbelief. 'I couldn't possibly leave, not now.'

'You don't look as though he's making you very happy,' said Mrs Soames, shrewdly.

Selina was in a spin. 'That's the problem,' she admitted. 'I don't know whether he is or he isn't.'

'One day you will know,' said Mrs Soames as she bustled around the stove.

Finally the bell rang and Selina returned to the dining room. Now the atmosphere in the room was positively electric, and as she bent to place the plate of veal before her master he cupped the undersides of her breasts as though he were weighing them in each hand.

'You simply couldn't wait, could you?' he said.

'I can't help it,' cried Selina. 'You've made me like this. My body's never quiet any more. I always seem to need something – something more than you let me have.'

Oliver tutted at her petulant outburst, and waited patiently for her to calm herself.

'That's the whole point of discipline,' he eventually condescended to say. 'It teaches you self-control.'

'But I shouldn't be like this,' she moaned. 'It's all wrong and wicked.'

'Wrong? There's no right or wrong about it. We're not hurting anyone, so why is it wrong?'

'I just know it is.'

'I do hope you're not going to develop a conscience,' said Oliver sarcastically. 'That would really spoil things.'

'What… what's going to happen to me?' she quietly ventured to ask, not really wanting to hear the answer.

'You and Jake will be visiting the dungeon after dinner,' he said, smiling at her as though that were a real treat. 'You'll both be punished. If anything, he knows the rules better than you do because he's been with me longer, although I can understand why he broke them. You are incredibly tempting. But he still has to learn that obedience is everything. He's lucky I'm not dismissing him, and if it weren't for Mary, I would.'

'Please, I don't want to go to the dungeon,' whimpered Selina.

'Then you should have resisted Jake,' Oliver countered conclusively. 'Now go back to the kitchen. When I've finished my meal I'll come for you. Mary's already taken Jake to be prepared, and they'll be waiting for us.'

He kept Selina waiting for over half an hour, and she prowled restlessly around the hallway, her mind and body churning with a mixture of excitement and genuine fear. By the time he came for her she could scarcely speak and was trembling from head to toe. He ran a hand down her spine, his fingers lingering at the cleft at its base.

'You feel like a nervous filly,' he said with a smile. 'Well, a good filly has to be broken in, and so do you. Time to go.'

As they crossed the stone bridge to the old wing of the house Selina saw someone approaching from the opposite direction, and realised that a visitor must have arrived and used the old entrance on the far side of the field.

'Oh no, it's the major!' she exclaimed in horror as they drew closer. 'He's an old friend of my father. What's he doing here?'

'I invited him over for a drink,' Oliver said casually, clearly enjoying her distress. 'Thought I'd better get acquainted with the locals, and the major seems to be the man with all the influence around here.'

'But… but he mustn't see me like this!' she gasped. 'What on earth's he going to think?!'

'How much you've changed, I would imagine,' Oliver sniggered flippantly, and then put an arm tightly round her waist and pulled her close.

As the major drew level with them he started to lift his hat and smile in greeting, before his brain registered that it was Selina and what she was wearing, and his eyes hungrily devoured her breasts, and his expression changed to one of total astonishment.

'Is that you, Selina?' he asked incredulously.

'Y-yes,' she blustered shamefully.

'Good evening, major,' Oliver greeted him cheerily, as though there was nothing extraordinary about Selina's attire. 'If you go on up to the house Mrs Soames will show you to my study and fix you a drink. I'll not be too long.' And then, smiling politely, he guided Selina on, leaving the major gawking at the space so recently occupied by the beautifully erotic vision, his hat hovering in mid-air.

Selina felt herself going scarlet with shame, but there was nothing she could do, and she wondered how long it would be before everyone in the village heard of her humiliation.

'I hope he enjoyed that,' said Oliver, lifting his nose and breathing deeply the evening scents. 'I expect you've grown since he last saw you,' and once more he laughed.

'Why do you enjoy humiliating me so much?' cried Selina.

'Because I get so aroused by you when you blush and tremble,' he replied, his hand suddenly urgent on her nipples, toying with them like a child with a plaything. 'It's such a shame that you have to be punished tonight,' he added. 'If only you'd been able to control your lust. Still, what's done is done, and no doubt the evening will be entertaining for us all.'

A few minutes later Selina was being guided down the metal steps into the dungeon. The first thing she saw was Jake, handcuffed to a high rail, hanging with his toes barely brushing the stone floor, his muscular body stretched and rippling with the strain.

'Here we are, Mary,' said Oliver jovially. 'Now they pay the price for their pleasure and deception.'

Mary's green eyes narrowed as she smiled back at him, while Selina's stomach clenched tightly with fear.

As she glanced apprehensively about, Oliver pushed her across the room and ordered her to lie down on a hard metal cot. Once she was lying there he spread her limbs, using buckle-cuffs with chain and dog-clip fastenings to secure her wrists and ankles to the metal frame. She struggled as he fastened her, knowing that once she was secure she would be unable to protect herself from anything he decided to do. But his strength was far greater than hers, and within a few minutes she was lying exactly as he wanted, and tears filled her eyes when he picked up a latex whip and drew it lightly over her ribcage.

'Please don't hurt me,' she begged.

'But it gives you such pleasure,' he goaded.

'Not always.'

'Really? I hadn't noticed that,' he sneered. 'Anyway, I don't intend to use this on you at the moment. I think Mary deserves some compensation for what you and Jake did in the kitchen, don't you?'

'Compensation?' Selina didn't understand him.

'But of course. She and Jake have been together for a long time. Mary's bound to feel hurt at his betrayal.'

Selina knew he was playing with her. She didn't believe for one moment that Jake and Mary were faithful to each other, but she couldn't possibly argue with the man standing over her so threateningly.

'Mary would like some pleasure herself,' he continued smoothly. 'Let's see how quickly you can give it to her.'

Selina lay tensely waiting to see what was going to

happen and then, as Mary crouched over her, settling herself so that she was sitting just above Selina's face, she knew what she had to do, and as the auburn girl lowered herself Selina began to use her tongue. Carefully she parted the other girl's sex lips, licking and sucking at the flesh until she felt Mary's juices start to flow.

Above her Mary squirmed in delight. 'Put your tongue inside me,' she ordered Selina. 'Taste my juices, spread them around, suck on my clit.'

Selina tried frantically to obey. Her tongue darted from Mary's vagina up the moist inner channel, and then circled the rapidly hardening bud she knew contained all the delicious nerve-endings. Mary began to cry out with pleasure, pressing down hard against Selina's mouth.

'Eat me,' she shouted. 'Suck me, devour me. Hurry… hurry!'

Selina was working as fast as she could, her tongue starting to ache as it constantly travelled back and forth, and then she touched Mary's perineum and heard her groan with delight. Inspired, Selina plunged her tongue inside the other girl's hot, damp opening and twirled it around before flicking it in and out, remembering how incredibly good it had felt when Kara had done that to her.

Now Mary was screaming with excitement, and then with gratifying speed her internal muscles tightened and her thighs closed around Selina's head as she spasmed furiously, her climax long and loud, and her cries of excitement rang around the dungeon.

As Mary's pleasure spilled over Selina's need grew and her hips shifted restlessly on the bed. The leather thong stuck to her damp sex lips, pressing on her own clitoris and causing tiny slithers of delight, like electric shocks, to shoot through her belly.

Oliver bent over her and began to stroke the creases at

the tops of her thighs, occasionally applying pressure to her outer labia, moving his fingers so that everything beneath them was stimulated. Now it was Selina's turn to whimper with rising excitement.

'Keep working on Mary,' said Oliver calmly. 'I want you to bring her off again, but you can't come yourself.'

'Then leave me alone,' gasped Selina from beneath the other girl's humid thighs. 'I'll come if you don't.'

'I trust you've learnt better than that by now,' he said harshly, and she tried frantically to subdue her quaking muscles. He knew her so well now that he was able to bring her to a frenzy within seconds, and soon her cries were as fervent as Mary's. But then, as Mary's body spasmed once more, Selina pressed down on her cramping muscles, knowing she was about to come and determined not to displease Oliver any more.

'That was very good,' remarked Oliver, when Mary had finished and Selina was lying, fully aroused but motionless, on the bed. 'Your self-control's definitely improving.'

Mary climbed dreamily off the bed, and Oliver readjusted Selina so that she was sitting up against the metal frame at the head, still fastened, and able now to see Jake. He was staring across the dungeon at her, his erection sprouting hugely from his groin, and she could smell the musky aroma of his arousal.

'Doesn't she look good, Jake?' asked Oliver. Jake nodded, and Selina wondered if he was too scared to answer. 'I expect you'd like to take her, to plunge yourself inside her and spill your seed,' continued Oliver. Again Jake nodded, and winced as even that slight movement caused terrible pressure on his straining shoulders.

'If you manage to control yourself while Mary works on you, then you can have her,' said Oliver casually. 'I'm sure that should provide a good incentive for you to resist.'

Jake looked hungrily at Selina, but his eyes were full of despair, and she knew that he doubted his ability to survive Mary's ministrations.

Now that she was being left alone for once, Selina watched with interest as Mary pushed a low stool in front of Jake and then stepped onto it to rub her naked body against his, her hands around his waist to keep him still. Selina was fascinated by the way Mary moved, the sinuous way she writhed up and down her lover's body, her tongue licking beneath his armpits where the skin was stretched so tightly, and her hands straying all over his chest. After long electric minutes, when only their heavy breathing and soft murmuring disturbed the dank silence, Mary stepped down from the stool, and as she moved it to one side Selina could see that Jake's erection looked painfully stiff. The tip was a glistening purple while his balls were pulled tight against his body, clearly ready to explode at any moment. His mouth twisted with passion, yet still he watched Selina with intense yearning. She knew that, at that moment, he wanted to possess her more than he wanted anything else. The realisation excited her beyond belief.

Sitting next to her on the bed, Oliver ran a possessive hand thoughtfully over her flesh. 'It turns you on, doesn't it?' he murmured. 'You like seeing him like that, tied up, aroused and desperate to have you, and yet knowing he never will.'

'He might,' Selina sighed.

Oliver shook his head. 'Mary will make sure he doesn't,' he said. 'She knows better than to allow him to have what he wants. It would displease me too, and that's something Mary would never do.'

His hands continued to move carelessly over Selina's body, and her breathing quickened as she watched Mary kneeling down in front of Jake, her mouth closing around his straining cock, her head bobbing up and down. All the time she worked Jake's muscles heaved and rippled with the strain, and Selina's excitement grew until she was ashamed of herself.

After several minutes Mary stopped what she was doing, and glanced over her shoulder at Oliver. 'I thought he'd have come by now,' she quietly confessed, looking apologetic.

'Clearly Selina's more of a temptation than you'd thought,' said Oliver. 'Either that, or you're losing your touch, Mary.'

Selina could see the cold remarks angered the auburn girl. Fury simmered in Mary's eyes as she picked up a small bottle and poured oil all over her lover's cock. For a few moments she manipulated him with her hands, and then, as his hips began to twitch and his chest swelled as he inhaled deeply, she moved behind him, and Selina realised she was spreading more oil over and between his buttocks. Then she moulded herself against him like a hungry feline, and slightly to one side so that Selina and Oliver could see what was happening, began to pump his cock with one fist, and jabbed a rigid forefinger into his lubricated rectum.

The air hissed from Jakes lungs. Despite his bonds he tried frantically to squirm away from her, twisting and turning, but she was remorseless and there was no escape. He cried out, but still he didn't come.

'You must want her very much,' Mary accused quietly. 'But I don't think you'll be able to survive this…'

Selina watched Mary release the swollen penis and reach back into the shadows. When her greased hand emerged from the gloom she was holding a monstrous vibrator, which she held for Selina and Oliver to see, but out of Jake's vision. With a wicked smile dancing on her lips, she lowered the gnarled implement, removed her finger and spread his buttocks, and then buried the plastic into his bottom with one long thrust. Jake tensed and tried to move his hips forward and away from the relentless invasion, but his cock was instantly enveloped in her slick fist again. He held still, and then his lips sagged and he groaned as Mary fiddled with the minimal piece of plastic which now protruded from between his hollowed buttocks, and Selina heard it start to buzz. His body began to shake violently as the dildo inside his tight back passage began to vibrate.

He appeared to be delirious, mumbling and groaning, denying the impending orgasm while his hips ground backwards and forwards as his body sought the satisfaction his mind was trying to suppress.

Selina's breasts ached and there was a dull throbbing between her thighs. She'd never seen a man so excited yet so unfulfilled before, and it was driving her frantic. Suddenly Jake shook uncontrollably and Oliver emitted a sigh of contentment as, with a terrible groan, Jake's body was racked by fierce orgasmic spasms and his sperm shot forth, arching high into the dank air and splattering audibly onto the cold stone floor of the dungeon.

'I didn't realise you fancied her so much,' taunted Mary, lightly fingering her lover's rapidly shrinking cock.

'Turn off the vibrator,' Jake begged her.

'No, I want to see you get hard again,' said Mary.

Oliver laughed sadistically. 'I wonder how long it will take,' he said thoughtfully to Selina. 'Perhaps this will help him,' and his hands were on her aching nipples and he was pulling them, pulling them so hard that she screamed with the pain of it. As she screamed she saw Jake tense, and his eyes fasten onto her and Oliver again. Oliver was pinching her nipples, imprisoning them in his fierce grip, and she started to arch off the cot.

'Remember, you can't come yet,' he whispered cruelly.

'Please let me,' she implored him. 'Please. Haven't I waited long enough?'

'This is just to arouse Jake,' explained Oliver, as though that made it all right. As Selina sought to subdue her own release she saw that Jake's cock was slowly beginning to harden again, and she could hear the hum of the diabolical vibrator as Mary moved it fiendishly in and out of his rectum.

'I bet that's hurting him,' remarked Oliver as Jake's erection grew. 'I doubt he'll ever touch you again after this.'

'I thought Mary was meant to love him,' whimpered Selina, squirming away from Oliver's hands as they continued to try and wrench an orgasm from her, an orgasm that was forbidden by him.

'I don't think I ever mentioned love,' said Oliver shortly.

Jake was beseeching Mary to leave him alone, to stop, and the more he begged the more excited Selina grew.

'Let him go now,' said Oliver suddenly, and Mary looked at her master in astonishment.

'But, why?' she asked, clearly angered.

'Because I say so.'

Selina could see how much Mary hated obeying the order, and she was pleased, because now the other girl was suffering too.

Once Jake was released he slumped to the floor, groaning and clutching himself, while Mary stood over him, her eyes clearly transmitting her annoyance and lack of pity.

'You can both go now,' said Oliver dismissively, turning his attention to the trussed beauty by his side. 'I shall finish here. The rest of Selina's punishment is between her and me. You did right to report what happened, Mary,' he said without looking at the auburn girl, 'and I trust you feel amply rewarded?'

'Yes, thank you, sir,' replied Mary, grudgingly. Almost certainly, Selina knew, the sadistic girl was annoyed that she wasn't being allowed to witness Selina's final punishment. But Selina was relieved; she didn't want her own maid to see her sobbing like Jake had sobbed.

'And now it's just the two of us,' said Oliver, as the other two climbed the ladder and closed the door behind them. 'You seem to be very excited, my dear. It's difficult to think of anything that will punish you without giving you pleasure, you're so near to coming.'

Oliver stood and gazed thoughtfully down upon Selina for a while. Then, seeming to make up his mind, he unfastened her wrists and roughly removed her body harness, before positioning her flat on her back on the cot and once again fastening her wrists and ankles to the four corners.

'I prefer you naked,' he muttered. 'It gives me more flesh to aim at.'

Selina flinched at his uncompromising words. 'Please, you're not going to beat me, are you?' she implored.

He sniggered. 'You'll just have to wait and see, now won't you?' And then he blindfolded her, slipping a thick black mask over her eyes, leaving her lost in darkness, tugging helplessly against her restraints.

She hardly dared to breathe as she waited for what was to come. The cellar was eerily silent. Either he was still standing over her, or he was moving around very quietly. Either way, it increased the tension so much that she began to shake.

It seemed like an eternity before she felt the first caress of the whip travelling around her breasts, the point circling each globe, and her breathing grew ragged. Despite the fact that she'd guessed what was coming before the first blow fell, burning into the soft and vulnerable flesh, she screamed with shock and pain. She knew there was no point in protesting, that Oliver would continue remorselessly, but the pain was so great that she couldn't stop herself.

He waited until the terrible searing sensation had died away and then, with cruel kindness, trailed the whip a little lower, tracing it over the contours of her ribcage. Selina pressed herself into the damp-smelling mattress, trying desperately to escape the blow that was about to fall, but it was impossible. He struck down again and the whip scored her poor flesh.

The pattern of teasing caresses followed by swift blows of the whip went on and on, and Selina cried out every time he struck. But despite the pain she could feel herself becoming more and more aroused, and to her shame, when the whip moved between her thighs she actually thrust her hips upwards, straining for the punishment he was about to mete out.

Oliver worked with meticulous care. He never struck her twice in the same place, and he varied the length of time between strokes so that she became confused, barely able to distinguish between the soft caressing which was deceptively relaxing, and the harsh blows that caused such torment. The confusion only increased Selina's desire, and she felt her body straining towards a climax, but the keen edge of the pain prevented her from physical release.

When the whip moved over her vulva, the tip lightly tickling her bottom, she grew frantic with fear. 'Not there,' she begged him. 'Please don't hit me there.'

But he could have been deaf for all the notice he took, for he used his free hand to part her sex lips, drawing the whip upwards, and she could feel it clinging to her shamefully moist flesh. She could also feel her clitoris swelling into a hard little nut. As the tip of the whip moved around the centre of her pleasure she gasped and her belly contracted as desire surged through her.

Even as her breasts swelled and her juices flowed she knew what was to come, and hopelessly beseeched him not to do it.

But it was no use.

At last, after keeping her waiting for such an agonising length of time, the whip cracked down into the most sensitive part of her soft feminine places, and she arched off the bed again as her body shrieked its protests.

'It seems I have managed to punish you without you coming,' he gloated, as she sobbed helplessly on the bed, staring into the darkness. 'Never mind, it will make the eventual pleasure all the greater.'

Selina heard him moving around the room, and turned her head, blindly trying to make out what he was doing. She heard noises, a chinking sound which meant nothing to her, and then a tap was turned on, before he returned and she felt him sit at the foot of the bed. She wished she could see him, and had a fair idea of what to expect next. But somehow the darkness added to the erotic charge, and her vulnerability merely increased her lust.

When his tongue first moved between her fleshy lips she gave a squeal of shock, because it was icy cold. And then he was opening her up and slipping an ice-cube into her clinging entrance, pushing it in as far as he could with the tip of his tongue, and she began to shake violently with the strange sensation. He popped several ice-cubes in, one after the other, and she could feel them slowly melting as they touched her scolding flesh. Then a finger was inside her, moving them around, making sure she was numbed as best he could.

'It must feel strangely cold,' he pondered, as she shivered. 'I'll have to see if I can warm you up.'

Then, just as her body was adjusting to the freezing sensation of the ice, she felt him inserting something else inside her. It was thin and rubbery, and without warning her vagina was sluiced with beautifully warm water, and the contrasting sensations were so wonderful that to her astonishment she erupted and cried out in explosive ecstasy.

'Tell me how it feels,' Oliver urged, his mouth close to her ear as she heaved and writhed on the bed. 'Tell me. What was it like?'

Selina didn't know how to begin to describe it. 'The… the ice was so *cold*,' she panted, as her emotions gradually subsided. 'B-but it was exciting too… And then when you put that warm liquid inside me, I thought I'd go mad...' She smiled weakly from behind the blindfold. 'It… it was lovely.'

'I promised you pleasure, now didn't I?' he said.

Through swirling emotions Selina thought she detected a softening in his voice, and also growing excitement. Instinctively, she started to move her hips, gently rotating and lifting them, silently urging him to continue pleasuring her in whatever way he chose. She heard his breathing quicken and felt a momentary sense of triumph when, within a few seconds, he was lying naked on top of her, his chest heavy against her breasts and his erection gliding up and down on her clitoris. She was still sore there from his spiteful blow, but soon her longing was rekindled, and he ground more firmly against her punished bud, pausing occasionally to press his bulbous tip just into her moist entrance.

Every time he did so Selina would panic a little, almost unable to contain her excitement, and then he would withdraw and resume moving up and down the moist channel, the head of his cock pushing back the protective hood of skin that was trying to cover her frantic clitoris.

She'd never felt his whole body moving against her like that before. It was more intimate than anything he'd previously allowed. She hoped it was a good sign, that perhaps he was beginning to feel something for her, but it was impossible to understand the workings of his mind, and she decided she must simply be content with the moment.

At last he eased inside her. To start with he only allowed the tip of his erection to slide in and out, and she tried her hardest to move so that she could take in more of him, but the metal restraints prevented her.

'Just wait,' he whispered against her ear, and immediately she obeyed.

He teased her mercilessly, moving around just inside her until she was so excited she began to cry with frustration, begging him to thrust deeper. Gradually, a fraction at a time, he allowed himself to sink further in. Then he withdrew totally, and as she gave a cry of anguish he dropped his hips and filled her with one smooth lunge. He ground his hips against hers, and they moaned together, gasping as the friction between their bodies aroused them to even greater heights, and Selina heard Oliver gasping as he tried to hold back.

'Grip me tighter with your muscles,' he encouraged hoarsely. 'Imagine you have to hold me inside you.'

His words and the feel of him pulsing deep within intensified her rapture. She was rapidly approaching the point of no return and started to mutter incoherently, and she knew she could no longer hold back.

Her orgasm crashed over her and she bucked insanely beneath his weight. Through spiralling mists of joy she heard Oliver grunt, and then felt him spilling his seed into her, before collapsing on her helpless and drained body. She could feel his heart pounding against her chest, and knew her own was racing too. He was heavy, but she didn't care. She didn't mind the discomfort, because for the first time there was physical closeness between them, and that gave her more pleasure than the orgasm itself.

Oliver lay still for several minutes, and Selina hardly dared breathe, terrified that she'd break the spell. When he eventually did move she wanted to reach up and pull him back to her, but her wrists were still tethered and she was powerless. He had total control over her, and she had to follow his lead.

'I'm really very pleased with you,' he eventually said, stroking her straining shoulders. 'You're doing much better than anyone's ever done before you.'

Selina didn't know whether to reply or not. She wanted to. She wanted to tell him how happy she was, that she wanted to be the best mistress he'd ever had – or have – but she remained silent, her intuition telling her that he would prefer her to remain so.

She felt his hands fumbling at the fastenings, and at last she was free. Her muscles complained and she winced as she sat up and slipped the blindfold off. Trying to ignore the aching in her limbs, she gazed around the room and blinked as her eyes readjusted to the gloomy light.

Oliver was already pulling on his clothes, not even bothering to look at her, and she wondered what lay in store when his friends from London came up for the weekend.

It seemed as though Oliver could read her mind. 'I hope you haven't forgotten we're having an open house this weekend,' he said casually.

'I haven't forgotten,' she responded meekly.

'Good. I want you to prepare everything. On Saturday

night we'll have a sumptuous dinner. Sunday breakfast will be a casual affair, naturally, and I expect most of them will return home late Sunday morning.'

'What time are they arriving?'

'Early Saturday afternoon. And they'll be anxious to see how I punish you for your mistakes during our visit to London.'

Selina's stomach lurched. 'But… but I thought you *had* just punished me.'

Oliver snorted derisively. 'Oh no. That was for what happened between you and Jake in the kitchen. On Saturday you're to be punished for your earlier misdemeanours.' He smiled arrogantly, before adding, 'I must say, I'm rather looking forward to Saturday.'

'W-what can I wear to go back to the house?' asked Selina, trying to avert her thoughts from the impending and probably humiliating punishment, and hoping she hadn't to put on the body harness again.

'You can wear this,' he said, throwing her a towelling robe. 'I think the body harness has served its purpose for today. Did you like wearing it?'

Selina thought for a moment. 'It… it did make me feel sexy,' she admitted with innocent honesty. 'But I didn't like it. I felt too exposed, too vulnerable.'

'That's exactly why I had you wear it,' said Oliver, satisfaction evident in his voice. 'I think we'll bring it out again on Saturday. My guests will enjoy the sight of you like that. You really do look incredibly tempting in it.'

As Selina pulled on the towelling robe she winced as the rough cotton fabric touched the places where the whip had fallen earlier. Glancing down at herself she saw that her body was covered in raised red stripes, which in the ecstasy of orgasm she'd almost forgotten about.

'Such lovely pale flesh,' murmured Oliver, running a

hand over the damaged skin. 'I think Georgina would enjoy taking a crop to you.'

'No, please…' whispered Selina, horrified at the very thought of that sadistic woman armed with a whip.

'If it's what I decide upon, then it's what will happen,' said Oliver firmly, and Selina's head fell forward as she trailed miserably out of the room, her previous delight at what had passed between them totally erased by his casual cruelty.

Chapter Ten

The next couple of days were frantically busy. Selina found there was a lot to do if the house was to be prepared according to Oliver's instructions. Her father had virtually never entertained at Summerfield Hall, and certainly not on the scale that Oliver intended to. As a result she decided to call in a firm of professional cleaners, because despite earlier efforts, a slightly musty air still lingered in some of the rooms.

Mrs Soames asked Selina's advice about all the menus, although Selina wished she wouldn't, as she was certain that the older woman knew more about Oliver's requirements in that respect than she did. However, she painstakingly worked out a dinner and a breakfast that she felt would ensure the guests' taste buds were appropriately stimulated, because she was in no doubt that Oliver intended the entire weekend to be one long hedonistic experience.

'Have you always worked in London?' she asked the housekeeper as they worked together.

'I prefer not to discuss my employment with Mr Richards,' Mrs Soames remarked bluntly.

'I'm sorry, but I know so little about him,' Selina explained.

Mrs Soames remained uncompromising. 'If he wanted you to know more then he'd tell you.'

'I suppose he thinks power is knowledge,' said Selina. 'As he needs to be in control all the time, the less other people know about him the better. He doesn't even discuss his work.'

'You must have heard about him during some of his famous cases,' exclaimed Mrs Soames. 'He's always defending the rich and famous, usually in libel actions.'

'I think I may have read about him once or twice, but my father and I rarely watched television.'

Mrs Soames glanced sideways at Selina. 'Don't assume that he's giving you a balanced view,' she said softly, and then pursed her lips as though annoyed with herself for saying too much.

Once the cleaners had gone Selina instructed Mary to make sure that every room had a large floral arrangement in it, using freshly cut flowers from the garden. 'It makes such a difference,' she told Mary, but the maid didn't reply. 'I want everything to be perfect,' continued Selina anxiously. 'I just know that this is a very important weekend for Oliver, and I don't want to do anything wrong that might spoil it.'

'I'm sure you don't, ma'am,' said Mary demurely, but there was nothing demure about the expression in her eyes.

On the Friday morning, as Selina hurried upstairs wearing her grey dress, she met Oliver on his way down.

'Busy?' he asked.

'Desperately,' said Selina, brushing some loose hair out of her eyes. 'It's fun though, I have to admit. I'm enjoying getting the house ready for the weekend. It's lovely to see the place coming alive again.'

'Rather like watching you,' Oliver observed, and Selina shivered. As they drew level he gently stroked her flushed cheek for a moment, and then both hands were wandering down over her body, touching her possessively through the course cotton fabric. Selina was instantly aroused, and she closed her eyes dreamily.

'You look incredibly sexy,' Oliver drooled huskily, moving onto a lower step. Then his hands moved down her legs, slowly at first, but with increasing urgency, until he grabbed the hem of her dress and lifted it, leaving her totally exposed.

'Lean back against the wall,' he commanded. Then, as he planted his hands on either side of her, she realised that he'd already unzipped himself, because his erection was pushing against her sex and she felt herself opening to receive him.

For a few seconds he allowed his glans to play over her clitoris, until her breathing became ragged and she thrust her hips forward, desperate to draw him inside her and feel the aching void filled with his glorious thickness. Oliver needed no second invitation. Within seconds he was moving swiftly and urgently, and the sheer naughtiness and impulsiveness of their coupling made Selina orgasm immediately. As she swooned Oliver's climax flooded through him, and even when his convulsions abated he remained buried to the hilt, his fingers digging into her shoulders and his eyes devouring her.

Selina stared back at him from beneath lowered lashes, and sensed that he was slightly disturbed by his inability to resist her, and that he didn't quite understand how it had happened.

'You should be locked up in a nunnery,' he muttered at last, as he withdrew from her. 'You're simply too tempting.'

Selina knew better than to answer him. She remained against the wall as he adjusted his clothing, and then he continued on down the stairs as though nothing more than a courteous 'good morning' had passed between them.

That afternoon, when Selina went out into the garden, lifting her face towards the hot summer sun, she saw with surprise that Jake was busy working in the courtyard outside the covered entrance to the front door. He was surrounded by a pile of wood, hammering furiously, and so intent on his work that he didn't even notice her approaching.

'What are you doing?' she asked curiously.

'Obeying Mr Richards' orders,' he said flatly.

Ever since Jake had been punished for touching Selina he'd studiously ignored her, lowering his eyes whenever she passed, and she realised he was afraid of what might happen if Mary reported him again.

'Is it a secret?' she asked.

This seemed to amuse Jake. 'Only to those who don't know,' he said sarcastically.

Selina wasn't going to question him further, particularly when he was taking such pleasure in her bewilderment, and so she walked away, but for some reason the memory of the pile of wood unsettled her for the rest of the day.

When dinner was finished that evening she went back outside to see what he'd done. A small raised platform, about three feet high, had been built with steps leading up to it on either side. On top of the platform there was a wooden construction in an H shape, and the cross section had two holes cut out of it. Wondering what on earth it could be, Selina went closer to examine it further, and to her surprise saw that towards the front of the platform, near the edge, another hole had been cut, and a little in front of the hole a shallow depression had been hollowed out. She had no idea what it all meant, but knowing Oliver, it didn't bode well for her, and her imagination conjured up scenarios which were too disturbing even to contemplate.

Later, when Selina was about to go up to bed, Mrs Soames told her that Oliver wanted to see her. He was waiting in his study, papers and law books strewn all over his desk, and looked up with a smile as she entered.

'I've just been around the house checking on everything,' he said. 'You've done an excellent job.'

'Thank you,' replied Selina. 'I know it's a very special weekend for you.'

'A very special weekend for us both,' he corrected.

Selina's pulse quickened. 'You mean, because I'm going to play host to your friends?' she asked.

'No, that's not what I mean. This is your full initiation into my world, Selina. By the end of the weekend we'll both know whether or not you suit me.'

'And whether you suit me,' said Selina.

Oliver looked amazed at her audacity. 'Excuse me?'

'I am free to go whenever I want,' Selina reminded him, wondering why she was suddenly feeling so brave. 'The agreement does have to be mutual.'

Oliver smiled patiently. 'Not necessarily. You might wish to stay even if you fail, but I wouldn't keep you.'

'I might pass and choose to go,' Selina countered.

Oliver looked at her thoughtfully. 'You really have changed, haven't you?' he mused. 'I'm not sure whether I approve of the new Selina.'

'I was only making sure I'd understood everything correctly,' she said, backtracking because she didn't want to displease him now, before the weekend had even begun.

'I believe we understand each other very well indeed,' said Oliver. 'It will be a difficult time, Selina. There will be occasions when you'll be pushed to the limits of your endurance. But I want you to know that I hope you stay the course. You've become quite special to me.'

Selina felt a warm surge of delight. That was exactly what she'd increasingly wanted to hear, what she'd hoped for, but even as her spirits rose he spoke again. 'Of course, I tire of things easily. Today's obsession can become a thing of the past very quickly.'

Selina guessed he was telling the truth, but she also felt he was trying to protect himself, protect himself from her, and she was now more determined than ever not to fail. 'I understand,' she assured him.

'Then we'll drink to the weekend,' he said, pouring her a glass of dry white wine. As she started to drink it he moved around the desk and unbuttoned the top half of her dress, pulling it back off her shoulders. At the same time he removed the glass from her hand and then eased the dress down further still, exposing her breasts and pinning her arms to her sides. 'Rest your head back,' he ordered hypnotically, and as she obeyed she felt the chilled wine trickling down between her breasts. Her skin tingled, and then Oliver was lapping at the wine, drawing it into his mouth and also spreading it sensuously around each breast in turn, circling them with his tongue and decreasing the circles until her burgeoning nipples were covered with the cold and slightly sticky drink.

Oliver started to suck at her nipples, his hands firmly on her waist, and she revelled in it, feeling herself swelling beneath his ministrations. And when her body started to tense he moved his hands to her breasts, pinching the sensitive flesh in the way she liked best.

Selina's excitement was so great that she knew she was going to come at any moment, and just as her climax started Oliver's mouth closed over hers and she realised he was passing the wine from his mouth into hers. It was incredibly erotic, and she drank from his mouth while his hands worked their usual magic on her aching breasts.

When she came her body shuddered violently, and Oliver's fingers pinched her nipples with the savage cruelty she so loved. And then he was pouring wine down her throat straight from the bottle, and it was splashing all over her, and he continued to lap at the spillage as though he wanted to devour her.

Just when she thought she was going to come again he uttered a sharp exclamation. Abruptly he pulled her dress back over her shoulders.

'Do yourself up,' he said harshly, 'and get to bed. You need plenty of sleep, because you'll have very little after tonight until our guests leave on Sunday.'

Confused by his swift change of mood, Selina left the study.

Before she fell asleep that night she went over and over what had happened, and felt certain that once more, just as he had on the stairs, Oliver had given her pleasure on the spur of the moment. Clearly he was angry with himself, and she trembled as she realised that although at first she'd thought she was gaining a victory, it could well work against her. If Oliver was angry with himself then he would take the anger out on her, and perhaps make sure that the weekend was even more difficult for her than he'd originally planned.

Chapter Eleven

Selina was delighted to find the sun shining when she awoke the following morning. Gazing out of her bedroom window at the clear blue sky and white fluffy clouds, and the hazy mist rising from the grass, she knew it was going to be a glorious English summer's day.

Oliver hadn't told her what to wear but, knowing that the guests weren't due to arrive until after lunch, she pulled on a fresh grey dress.

As soon as she got to the kitchen Oliver appeared. 'I've sent for Georgina,' he announced. 'I've decided that I didn't care for your tone last night. You seem to have forgotten who owns Summerfield Hall, and I think you need reminding.'

Selina was horrified. 'But all the guests will be arriving after lunch,' she exclaimed. 'Does this mean I'll be needed earlier?'

'You certainly will,' confirmed Oliver. 'Wait in your room until I send for you. The staff can take care of anything that's still to be done.'

Perched on the edge of her bed, her arms wrapped round her knees, Selina waited miserably for nearly an hour. Then Mary came into the room and silently handed Selina an ivory-coloured lace chemise with matching silk knickers. 'You're to come down to the drawing room wearing these and nothing else,' said the maid.

Quickly Selina changed her grey uniform for the silken undergarments and then, with her head held high, she passed Mary, walked down the stairs and into the drawing room. Oliver was standing by the window with his back to her, while Georgina stood on the opposite side of the room, with Kim and Kara on either side of her.

'I expect you're looking forward to the weekend,' Georgina said.

'Very much,' replied Selina, as politely as she could.

Georgina turned to Oliver. 'You say she answered you back last night?'

'Yes.' His tone was abrupt.

'She seems subdued enough this morning.'

'That's only because I told her you were arriving early,' he explained. Walking over to one of the large armchairs he sat down, and then motioned for Selina to join him. Once she was settled on his lap he nodded to the waiting Georgina. 'You can start now,' he said.

Georgina pushed the two Thai girls in front of her and ordered them to strip. Selina noticed that the girls were almost identical in height and appearance, the only difference was that Kara had long hair. She watched as Georgina produced a thick leather strap which she proceeded to fasten around the two girls, so that their naked bodies were pressed together and they stood face to face waiting to see what was expected of them. Selina realised she was leaning forward eagerly on Oliver's lap, and she felt a hand tickling the crease of her left thigh, moving up inside the leg of her silk knickers, but he too was watching Kara and Kim.

'You can take it in turns to bring each other off,' said Georgina. 'I don't mind what order you go in, but I expect you both to keep busy until I tell you to stop. And no faking it, I'll know if you do.'

No sooner had she spoken than the two girls lay, with surprising ease considering the way they were trussed, on the floor. The belt clearly made it awkward for them, but within a few seconds Kara was lying on top of Kim, her long hair brushing the other girl's upper arms and shoulders, and her hands moving rapidly over Kim's breasts, her fingers delicately caressing the golden skin.

Selina could clearly see Kim's childlike nipples beginning to grow, and she felt a thrill of excitement as the Thai girl's movements increased.

Clearly Kara had played this game previously, for she was quick to slip one leg between Kim's and then use her upper thigh as a way of stimulating the other girl's entire vulva. Kim was uttering tiny sounds of excitement as the gentle fingers of her tormentor slid over her body, sensually touching her small breasts. And then Kara's tongue licked back and forth across them.

Kim was whimpering, her body straining and tightening, and Selina could imagine only too well how she was feeling as her pleasure mounted. When Kara's mouth fastened around Kim's nipple, Selina's nipples ached and yearned for a similar caress. Oliver's fingers now strayed into Selina's pubic hair, gently tugging while his thumb moved with extraordinary lightness over her clitoris, which was pushing upward through her rapidly swelling and separating sex lips.

'This is exciting you, isn't it?' he murmured, and she hung her head in shame as her juices coated his fingers and confirmed his assessment.

With a surprisingly harsh sound Kim came, and immediately the two girls rolled over so that now Kara was underneath and it was Kim's turn to arouse her. Her hands moved more quickly than Kara's had done, and her mouth gobbled greedily at Kara's rigid little nipples. But instead of easing a thigh between Kara's, Kim used hers to squeeze Kara's together, and then she rocked from side to side and her weight drove the girl beneath her into ecstasy.

Within a few minutes Kara's body spasmed and rippled as her pleasure spilled forth. Selina's belly felt so tight she thought it would burst, but she was forced to continue watching as the girls rolled around the carpet, coming time after time, their pleasure seeming to increase with every orgasm.

Oliver had surreptitiously freed his erection, and Selina could feel it brushing between the cheeks of her bottom, pulsing against the tiny cleft at the base of her spine. His fingers continued to titillate her, but never enough to release the blissful spasms she craved. Instead he kept her permanently on the edge of satisfaction, every nerve-ending yearning for release as she watched the two girls being constantly satisfied.

Eventually the Thai beauties began to tire. Georgina watched them for a while. 'You're taking a long time, Kimmie,' she said softly, and Selina saw Kim immediately push her hips upwards, straining to force an orgasm, but to no avail. 'I can see I'll have to help you,' continued Georgina. 'Kneel up, both of you.'

Oliver was still relentlessly teasing Selina. Time and time again she was certain that she was about to tumble over the abyss, to be swamped by a wonderful release. But Oliver was too too skilful, and each time his fingers would become still and the pleasure would ebb a little, leaving her stranded and despairing.

Selina watched Georgina advance upon her two playthings clutching a long latex probe in each hand. Without pausing she slid these between the cheeks of the girls' bottoms, before turning on the power. The hapless girls responded instantly, arching back so that their breasts rubbed together, and they began to squirm helplessly as the anal probes started to reignite their exhausted bodies.

It no longer seemed to matter which of them came first, they were both overwhelmed with need, and without realising it Selina started to respond to the erotic display by shifting restlessly on Oliver's thighs. His hands gripped her waist and she found herself being manoeuvred, lifted, and then pressed down inexorably onto his standing erection. Sweet breath hissed from her lungs in unison with the movement, until her buttocks rested on his groin and she was filled completely. His fingers moved back to her clitoris, and she shuddered with the blissful realisation that she was finally to be allowed to come.

In front of her, Kara and Kimmie were being swamped by rhythmic muscular contractions as their continuing orgasms rolled over them. The sight of their writhing bodies provided Selina with even more stimulation, and she felt the heavy pulse stirring between her thighs, and gave a tiny sigh of relief.

Then, with horror, she realised that this was her undoing, because Oliver immediately lifted her, continuing to stimulate himself between the cheeks of her bottom, but leaving her totally bereft. And then she felt him coming copiously over the bare flesh of her lower back, just as the two Thai girls screamed again in ecstasy.

While Oliver rested his head against Selina and the two exhausted girls collapsed in a heap on the carpet, Georgina smiled without warmth at Selina. 'That should have prepared you for Oliver's visitors,' she said.

Selina couldn't believe she was being tormented so cruelly. At that moment she craved fulfilment more than anything. 'Please,' she whimpered, 'don't leave me like this.'

'You'll have plenty of satisfaction later on,' said Oliver. 'I just wanted to get you in the mood.'

Tears of frustration filled Selina's eyes. 'My breasts are

aching,' she moaned.

'If you don't keep quiet they'll ache even more, and it won't be a pleasant ache,' threatened Oliver, and Georgina's eyes sparkled with interest.

'Let me use my whip on them,' she suggested hungrily.

Selina shrank back against Oliver, scared to utter another sound in case she annoyed him more and Georgina got her wish.

He paused for a moment, a moment that seemed an eternity to Selina. 'I think not,' he said at last. 'I don't want her marked before my guests arrive.'

'That's a pity, I'd have enjoyed it,' said Georgina, with a look that transmitted her confidence that she would eventually get her wish, and then she turned her attention to Kim and Kara. 'I'll take these two to the dungeon. They enjoyed themselves too much.'

Oliver laughed, but Selina couldn't believe her ears. The girls had been ordered to come, to keep coming, and that was what they'd done. Georgina was going to punish them for obeying her. Not only that, but she could well imagine that Georgina's punishment was going to be extremely severe.

'Come along girls,' said Georgina briskly. 'You know perfectly well you overstepped the mark. Don't think you're going to get away with it, because you're not.'

As they were led out of the room, still fastened together and awkwardly shuffling sideways, Kim and Kara raised their eyes to Selina. Selina couldn't quite read the message there. She couldn't make out if they were sorry for themselves or for her, but she had the dreadful suspicion it was for her.

Alone with Oliver, Selina continued to sit on his lap, awaiting his instructions. Eventually he pushed her off and watched dispassionately as she tumbled to the floor. 'Get yourself a light lunch, and then Mary will dress you in your body harness,' he said.

'Do I *have* to wear that?' she asked, her voice tight with fear.

Oliver looked at her thoughtfully. 'Maybe not,' he said. 'Perhaps we should go for something more original. It will have to be practical of course, and suited to the purpose, but I'm sure I can think of something.'

Selina wanted to ask him what purpose that was, but she didn't dare. Instead, she obeyed his next gruff order and left the room, remembering to walk with her head high, and trying to ignore the desperate sexual tension that screamed for release.

Georgina was not happy. She gazed at the pile of clothes in the middle of her bed and uttered an angry exclamation. She simply couldn't decide what to wear for the afternoon's entertainment, but that wasn't the true cause of her annoyance. The true cause of her annoyance was Selina.

'Do be quiet,' she said sharply, glancing to the corner of the room where Kim and Kara were standing against the wall, their wrists tied behind their backs and their bodies showing only too clearly the marks of their time in the dungeon.

Kim fell silent but Kara continued to utter the occasional sob. Walking across to them, Georgina grasped the girl's chin between strong fingers and stared into her eyes. 'Do you want another enema?' she threatened.

Kara shook her head, the fear flaring deep in her eyes.

'I thought not,' Georgina mused smugly. 'In that case, be quiet.' She allowed her hands to roam over Kara's abused body, caressing the raised marks. Then she parted the girl's slim buttocks, slipping a forefinger between them and into her rectum, where she rotated it thoughtfully for a few moments.

Kara, too wary of the woman to utter any sounds of protest, stiffened as her tortured flesh was forced to endure yet more humiliation and stimulation.

'Come for me,' coaxed Georgina. 'I want to see you come.' Her finger continued its relentless probing, and then she knelt down and began to lick the girl's lower belly, occasionally nipping at the delicate flesh with her teeth. After a short time the dusky beauty's pleasure started to simmer and grow.

'That's better,' said Georgina approvingly, 'but I can't wait, so hurry up.'

It was obvious to Georgina that Kara was trying her utmost to obey, but her exhausted body was betraying her, failing at the vital moment. Finally losing patience, Georgina reached up and tugged hard on one of the tiny nipple rings. Kara threw back her head with an anguished cry, but even as she did so the rhythmic contractions began and Georgina sighed with satisfaction as the wretched girl's orgasm was finally delivered.

Tiring of her toy, Georgina prowled restlessly around the room. She couldn't understand why Selina had got under her skin so badly. Normally she enjoyed helping Oliver train a new girl, enjoyed being part of the initiation of a mistress, but she wasn't enjoying it with Selina. She was beginning to realise that subconsciously she'd always wanted the girls to fail. When Lisette had lost her courage and asked for her freedom, Georgina had been delighted. It wasn't that she wanted Oliver for herself, since she wasn't submissive there'd be no point, but she'd always felt that she was closer to him than any other woman. Because Oliver was so intelligent and because their careers were both in law, they had a lot in common, and she'd never really felt their closeness had been threatened by any other girl.

Until now.

Selina was different. Despite the fact that the training sessions had all been similar to previous ones, Georgina sensed that Oliver felt differently about her. If she hadn't known him better, she'd have thought he really cared for her; that he was involved on an emotional as well as a physical level. If that were true and Selina passed all the tests, then Georgina would lose her privileged position, because Oliver would no longer need her.

Of course she'd still be invited to his parties, still be involved in most of his sexual depravities, but it wouldn't be the same. She was the only woman he'd ever listened to, the only woman he trusted enough to discuss his innermost secrets with, but now Selina was threatening to change everything – and Georgina didn't like that.

With a sigh of irritation she picked up one of the previously discarded dresses. What she wore wasn't as important as what she did, she knew. However skilled Selina was, and however desperate to keep Oliver happy, Georgina didn't believe she was any match for her. As long as Georgina played her cards right she, with her vast wealth of sexual experience and cunning, would be able to oppress and defeat the relatively naïve daughter of Hugh Swift.

She suddenly had a wonderful vision of Oliver handing Selina over to her. She imagined what it would be like to see the girl suspended, her body shaking, not from desire but from pure terror, as Georgina was allowed, at last, to use the whip on her. That was certain to happen at some point over the weekend, and that would be her opportunity to ensure that Selina failed. It was obvious that Selina was frightened of her, and up until now Oliver had, for some reason, protected the girl. But during the weekend he wouldn't be protecting her from anything, which would give Georgina a chance to make certain that Selina didn't become a permanent fixture in Oliver's household.

At last a smile played across Georgina's lips, and as her mood lightened she returned to the two Oriental girls.

'I'm going to untie you now,' she said, 'and lie on the bed while the both of you pamper me. I want to be totally relaxed before the entertainment begins this afternoon.'

The girls knew Georgina so well that it took them no time at all to bring her to a peak of excitement. Kim concentrated on Georgina's full breasts and turgid nipples, while Kara worked between the long slender thighs, using both fingers and tongue. Soon Georgina was squirming beneath the wonderful sensations as her two playthings obediently brought her to one climax after another, until she could take no more and had to finally stop them.

'That was *lovely*,' she purred approvingly. 'I'll probably need at least one of you later. You've been very good girls.' She kissed them briefly, her fingers pinching their soft breasts, and then she dressed and went downstairs.

She no longer felt angry or depressed. Now she felt in control again, certain that by the end of the weekend Selina would have fled from Summerfield Hall, just as all her predecessors had fled from Oliver's demands. Then he'd begin again with another girl, and Georgina would still be the only woman he really trusted.

She couldn't wait for the moment when she had Selina at her mercy.

Chapter Twelve

'Very nice,' Oliver murmured approvingly as Selina walked into the drawing room at two o'clock that afternoon. 'The dress is perfect. Mary has excellent taste.'

Selina didn't reply. She'd already seen herself in the mirror in her bedroom. The black and white polka dot cotton dress had narrow shoulder straps, and was so short she was only decent if she stood perfectly straight. Her legs were bare, shaved smooth and then made soft by the perfumed body lotion that Mary had rubbed into them. On her feet she wore black open-toed sandals, and for some strange reason she felt more vulnerable than if she'd been in the body harness. At least, when wearing that, everything was on display. Somehow, with a dress that just covered everything the effect was more erotic, and since she was naked beneath it no one would have any trouble in touching and arousing her.

'I think it needs one finishing touch,' continued Oliver, holding out his hands. Selina's heart sank as she saw a thin black leather collar, and then he was fastening it around her throat and clipping a leash to it.

'Exquisite,' he adjudged at last, running one finger around the inside of the collar. 'My guests will adore you.'

There was nothing Selina could say or do; nothing except wait and see what the coming hours held in store for her.

Oliver's eyes darkened. 'Good luck,' he said in a sinister tone that made the girl shudder, and then he led her out of the room and into the hall, where Mary was waiting.

'Take her outside,' he instructed the maid. 'When my

guests start arriving, hand her over to whomever wants her.'

Selina looked piteously at him. 'When will I see you again?' she asked.

'I'll be here all the time,' he replied, and then was gone.

Outside it was very hot indeed, yet Selina felt cold with fear. Already she was horribly nervous, and no one had yet arrived. What on earth would she be like when they did?

Mary paraded her around the edge of the lawn for a while, and Selina was aware that Georgina was watching, accompanied by the two Thai girls, while from one of the many borders Jake glanced up from his labours, and then quickly down again and got on with his work.

A few minutes later a dark car drew smoothly up the crunchy drive and stopped outside the house. Selina recognised the couple that climbed out. It was Harry with his wife, Charlotte.

Harry looked over at Selina. 'Hello there!' he called, waving cheerfully. 'Nice to see you again.'

'Such a lovely day!' added Charlotte.

Selina didn't know what to do. They sounded so normal, so matter-of-fact, and yet she was being led around like a slave girl.

'You're the hostess,' hissed Mary, tugging on the leash. 'You should respond.'

'H-hello,' called Selina, feeling utterly self-conscious and searching for something reasonable to say. 'Did – did you have a quiet drive up?'

'Perfectly,' Harry assured her, as he and his wife strolled across the lawn towards her. 'Looks as though some others are arriving,' he added, and Selina saw that cars were rolling up in a steady stream. The drivers and passengers were quick to get out and start milling around, stretching their legs. Their exaggerated greetings made it clear that they were all familiar with each other. Only Selina was new to most of them.

'Where's Oliver?' Charlotte asked her.

'Inside, I think,' she said vaguely, distracted by all the newcomers.

'I'll go in and see him,' said Charlotte eagerly. Reaching up she wound her arms around Harry's neck, and the pair kissed intimately for several seconds, and then with a giggle Charlotte pulled away and ran into the house.

'Give the lead to me,' Harry said to Mary, and the auburn girl immediately obeyed.

'Love the dress,' said Harry, running his free hand with infuriating arrogance over the material covering Selina's breasts. 'Nothing on underneath, I hope?'

Selina shook her head.

'Thought not. Oliver certainly knows how to train his girls. Let's have a look at one of those gorgeous tits then.'

As Harry spoke he tugged at one of the thin straps, pulling it down Selina's arm until the material fell away from her breast, revealing it to his hungry gaze.

With little finesse he casually fondled it for several minutes, pulling her closer to him with the leash, before finally lowering his head and kissing her forcefully on the mouth.

Selina felt his tongue worming its way between her lips, before she parted them and allowed it to thrust into her mouth, and all the time his hand continued massaging her breast.

Selina didn't like Harry. She wasn't attracted to him in the least, so it was doubly shaming to feel her nipples hardening under his touch. Harry was clearly delighted by her response.

'Quick off the mark, aren't you?' he muttered. 'Now,

don't you think you should do your hostess bit and demonstrate just how pleased you are to see me again?'

Before she could ask him what he meant, his hand moved to the back of the collar, beneath her hair, and he forced her to her knees. 'Unzip me,' he ordered.

Selina realised immediately what the man wanted, and fumbled awkwardly with his trousers. As the zip lowered she couldn't quite believe the speed at which events were unfolding; Harry and Charlotte had only arrived a few minutes before, and she was already about to take his penis in her mouth!

She became aware that others had joined the bizarre scene. Peeping up she saw Georgina watching her, and there was Christian and Jilly too. The knowledge that Christian had arrived and was now watching her on her knees, her fingers curled around his friend's pulsing erection, threw her for a few seconds.

She hesitated for a fatal moment.

Georgina's crop rose and fell with incredible speed, and Selina yelped as it cut spitefully across her shoulders. Needing no further prompting, she immediately drew Harry's swollen helmet into her mouth and raised a hand to grasp his rigid stem. Her head bobbed up and down, and she could feel the excitement of the onlookers.

'Move faster,' Harry ordered. Selina was anxious to obey quickly because she was so frightened of being hit by Georgina again. As a result her teeth lightly grazed the skin of Harry's sensitive glans, and he immediately thrust two fingers inside her collar, pulling her head away from him as she gasped and coughed. 'Hasn't he taught you not to bite?' he demanded.

'Naughty girl,' said Georgina quietly. Scarcely were the words out of her mouth before the whip bit into Selina's tender flesh again. Once more she cried out with pain, and she could tell that her pain was exciting the small audience.

'Try again,' suggested Harry, releasing her so that she gasped, relieved to be able to breathe freely once more. Swiftly she resumed sucking and licking him, until she tasted the first drops of salty fluid and knew he was very near to ejaculating. 'I'm going to come,' he confirmed, panting through gritted teeth. She closed her eyes and pumped him in her fist, and as his thighs trembled against her breasts her mouth filled with his copious eruption.

His penis was removed instantly, almost contemptuously, and she heard his zip being raised. When she opened her eyes he was once again the picture of normality, shaking Christian's hand and then giving Jilly a courteous peck on the cheek.

Only Georgina was still paying her any attention, gazing down at her, with a glint in her eye and a slight smile curling her rouged lips.

'Everyone enjoying yourselves?' asked Oliver, emerging from the house with his arm around Charlotte, and moving to greet his guests in the pleasant sunshine.

Selina stared at him from where she knelt on the lawn, her dress askew and her breast still naked. She wondered if he had any idea what Harry had just done to her.

Despite the warmth of the afternoon, a shiver ran down her spine when he turned and looked at her knowingly, as though reading her thoughts.

'You look as though you've been having a good time, Selina,' he said. 'Now you pay the price for your errors last week.

Chapter Thirteen

For some reason Selina instinctively looked at Christian as Oliver took the leash and lifted her to her feet.

'It's no good looking to him for help,' he said, tugging her sharply forward. 'He's only a visitor. I'm the one you obey.'

'What are you going to do to me?' she asked timidly.

'Jake's built this especially for you,' he said, indicating the wooden frame. 'Now, I think we'll have the dress off.' As he spoke he pulled the flimsy garment over her head, leaving her totally naked apart from her shoes, and a murmur of approval floated from the watching visitors.

Selina was pulled awkwardly onto the raised wooden platform, from where she stared down at everyone, her cheeks scarlet with distress.

'Lift your head,' Oliver commanded. 'You're supposed to look like my proud mistress, not some pathetic waif.'

'Then you shouldn't keep humiliating me,' she whispered defiantly.

'But you enjoy it,' he taunted, casually fondling her between her thighs, and encountering undeniable signs of arousal. 'Let's hope you enjoy this just as much,' he said, menacingly. He pointed to the hole in the wooden frame. 'Sit in that and rest your feet in the groove at the front edge of the platform.'

As soon as Selina obeyed she realised what the H-shaped structure was for. The holes in the crossbar were now level with her breasts. Sure enough, Oliver methodically lifted each pliable globe of flesh and eased them through the round apertures. It was a tight fit, and as she felt the compression of the restraint around her breasts she wriggled, and then realised with despair that her vulva and buttocks were hanging down beneath the platform, totally exposed to the tiny audience.

Just when she thought her humiliation could be no greater, Oliver fastened her ankles together and then forced her forward a little and tied her wrists to her ankles. She was now utterly defenceless.

'Do what you like with her during the rest of the afternoon,' Oliver called to his watching friends. 'Take your pleasure how you will. As she's being punished, she isn't allowed to enjoy an orgasm. If she does, I shall have to discipline her.'

At first it seemed that everyone was content to simply ogle her, but then they drew nearer. Selina stared blankly ahead, trying to shut her mind to the humiliations that lay in store.

'Can we use sex toys?' Jilly asked Oliver. 'She has such gorgeous breasts. I want to use a stimulator on them.'

'Use anything you like.'

'It's in the car – I'll be back in a jiffy,' Jilly excitedly assured the poor trussed girl. Selina wondered if Jilly really thought that was what she wanted to hear. She waited, feeling the sun beating down on her, and then Oliver lightly stroked her warm skin.

'We can't have you burning,' he said, with paradoxical tenderness. 'I'd better put some suntan oil on you.'

'Please don't do this to me,' she begged him. 'I've tried to do everything you've taught me. I've tried to please you.'

'Trying isn't enough,' he retorted, and then she felt his hand moving over her, spreading soothing oil across every inch of her skin. His touch was like a true lover's, tender and yet arousing, and she wished it was always like that.

'I know what you're thinking,' Oliver whispered to her. 'You wouldn't really like it though. You'd get bored. You're body needs more. I've trained you too well for you to be satisfied with an ordinary lover.'

In her heart of hearts Selina suspected he was right, that her debased flesh had been too finely tutored, and she was shamed by the knowledge.

'Here we are,' cried Jilly, hurrying back. She climbed up onto the platform to stand next to the imprisoned Selina, sitting helplessly in a modern version of the stocks. 'You'll just *love* the feel of this,' Jilly assured her. 'You're bound to come, because your breasts are so sensitive. I noticed that earlier.'

'But I'm not allowed to come,' Selina said despairingly.

'And that's the fun, isn't it!' cried Jilly. Swiftly she placed a clear plastic cup over Selina's imprisoned right breast. Leading from the cup was a piece of rubber tubing with a rubber ball at the end. The malleable cup clamped tightly over Selina's soft flesh. Jilly started to squeeze the bulb, and immediately Selina's breast began to firm and tighten and her nipple to throb as the vacuum suction drew blood into the area.

'It vibrates too,' giggled Jilly, touching a small button on the underside of the cup. Instantly Selina's breast started to tremble and she tried to pull away from the delicious torment, but Jake's handiwork was too good to allow that.

Harry was standing on the ground before her. 'She's going to come in a moment,' he announced enthusiastically, and Selina cringed as he stooped and reached beneath the platform and slipped a finger inside her. 'I'll tell you when she does,' he added.

'I think we'll all know,' Jilly assured him.

Selina was gasping now, trying with all her strength to subdue the passion that was rising within her. She couldn't believe how quickly she was being aroused, how exciting the titillation was, and she struggled to ignore her mounting pleasure.

'Isn't she sweet,' cried Jilly. 'I remember Lisette gave in much more easily than this, Oliver.'

'Selina's in a class of her own,' he replied, proudly.

'I think this is going to be the best weekend we've ever had,' said Jilly, pumping the bulb once more.

Selina gasped. It didn't seem possible that her breast could swell any more. The sensitive skin was so swollen that it was pressing hard against the covering and her nipple had never felt so rigid.

'You want to come, don't you?' murmured Jilly. 'Let it go… let your pleasure go. You can't stop it, not unless I leave you alone, and I'm not going to.'

Selina bit on her lower lip, trembling and quaking as her climax drew inexorably nearer.

'Any minute now,' called Harry, and his words tipped her over the edge. Suddenly Selina lost her battle and the rhythmic contractions pulsed through her as she exploded with rapture.

After a few silent minutes Oliver tutted like a disappointed parent. 'What a shame you had to let yourself down, Selina,' he admonished, but his tone made a lie of his words.

For a while Selina's torment eased a little. Oliver and his guests talked and enjoyed the refreshing drinks offered to them by Mrs Soames and Mary. Occasionally they would mill around and caress her idly, their hands straying over her breasts or between her sex lips. They all seemed amused and interested by her predicament, but none of them seemed desperate to force her to climax, and she found it quite easy to subdue the small tingles of excitement their touching aroused. Just as she was beginning to recover a little,

Christian spoke.

'I wish I'd brought my camera,' he said casually.

'Pictures aren't allowed,' replied Oliver.

Christian smiled confidently. 'I know the rules,' he said.

'Hm, that makes a change.' Oliver sounded genuinely annoyed. 'You never keep to them in court.'

'He's afraid he's going to lose his next case,' Christian explained to the imprisoned Selina, who was barely aware of their squabbling. 'He hates to lose at anything, don't you Oliver?'

'No more than you.'

'I suppose I'd better do my bit,' Christian remarked. Selina looked at him. His face was so deceptively kind, the soft brown eyes gentle and reassuring, but she knew better than to trust him. If he were what he seemed he wouldn't be there. 'I thought I'd use this,' he said.

Selina whimpered as Christian tapped a spatula-shaped piece of latex rubber against the palm of his hand. It was attached to a stocky handle, and she could imagine what it would feel like against her skin.

'I must say, you've got her in a very good position,' Christian conceded, whilst reaching beneath the platform.

'I'm glad you approve,' said Oliver, but there was no warmth there.

'Here we go then,' announced Christian, and then he struck the first blow. He hit Selina's left buttock and she screamed, unable to prevent herself from doing so. Even before the pain had died away Christian struck again, just to the side of where the first blow had landed. Once more she screamed, unable to believe how much it hurt. Christian seemed encouraged by her cries, and soon both buttocks were throbbing agonisingly.

'Please… please stop,' she sobbed.

'I can't,' he said reprovingly. 'We haven't reached the

pleasure stage yet.'

Selina continued to sob as Christian beat her remorselessly but skilfully, until the forbidden pleasure started to flicker and glow behind her pubic bone.

'I think she's enjoying it now,' adjudged Oliver.

Selina felt Christian pinch her left nipple. He didn't pinch it as hard as Oliver usually did, but it was hard enough to hurt, and the shaming pleasure was threatening to swamp her. She thought she'd go mad. Her body, desperate for release, continued its climb towards orgasm, and her head lolled back as the forbidden contractions began.

'No…' she pleaded helplessly.

'Yes,' mocked Christian, hitting her again with the latex crop. It was all too much for Selina's self-control. Racked by spasm after spasm of delicious pain-filled bliss, she felt her muscles pulsating relentlessly until once more she slumped exhausted against the wooden crossbar.

'You really do take immense pleasure from your punishment, don't you?' remarked Oliver. He gently stroked the damp hair from her perspiring brow, but she was already too weary to respond in any way. 'Keep your head up,' he said sharply. 'People are watching you.'

'I… I can't bear it any more,' she panted. 'I think I want to go.'

Oliver stroked the nape of her neck and leaned down to kiss her there. 'Are you sure?' he asked, his voice low and sensuous.

She wanted to scream with frustration. 'No…' she admitted. 'I'm not sure.'

'Then, you want to stay?'

'I… yes,' she blurted. 'But it's all your fault.'

'We must all take responsibility for our own actions,' he said, but kindly. 'There's nothing to be ashamed of. In fact, you should be proud of yourself.'

As the afternoon wore on Selina found that despite the shame and discomfort her ability to absorb pleasure seemed to increase. The novelty of the situation slowly wore off for the guests, and after a time they would simply wander across to her in ones and twos, their hungry hands and mouths devouring her. As she gained in confidence, Selina found that sometimes they didn't even bring her close to orgasm. At other times, even when they did, she was able to subdue the feeling.

'You're even more depraved than I'd imagined,' Oliver whispered proudly, as the sun lost its potency and the guests gradually drifted indoors to bathe and dress for dinner. 'You should be ashamed of yourself.'

And then his mood changed yet again, and he said, 'I'll get Jake to release you now. It's time for you to rest a little, and then to get ready for the evening.'

'I just don't know how all this could have happened,' Selina sulked. 'If I'd never met you...'

'You'd have had a very boring life,' he summed up for her, and then was gone.

Selina watched him walk to the house, and she asked herself yet again what had happened to turn her into the creature she'd become.

'Was it a good fit?' asked Jake, as he climbed onto the platform and began to unfasten the crossbar that was encasing her breasts.

'You'd better ask Oliver,' she said.

'I wish I'd been allowed to touch you,' he said furtively. 'I've been turned on all afternoon. You drive me out of my mind.'

'Do you want to get us into more trouble?'

'Of course not,' he said. 'But it's not my fault.'

The words had a familiar ring to them. Selina looked at him thoughtfully. 'But it *is* your fault,' she countered.

'We're all responsible for our own behaviour.'

Jake was clearly taken aback by her attitude. 'I don't know why you're so full of yourself.' He was fumbling with the straps at her ankles now. 'Just wait until he tires of you. He always tires of his women, unless they leave first. The ones he tires of he gives to Mary and me. I hope that's what happens with you.'

'If he tires of me, then I'm free to go,' said Selina. 'He hasn't the right to hand me to anyone else.'

'It would be his parting gift,' insisted Jake.

Selina didn't know whether to believe him or not, or quite what he meant. She had an awful feeling that he might be telling her something. If he was, then she knew that her final moments at Summerfield Hall would probably be some of her worst.

Jake finished releasing the bonds and helped her to her feet. 'Enjoy your dinner,' he said sarcastically, and then trudged away.

As Selina stretched and eased her cramped body, rubbing her aching muscles, she realised there was no one else left in the shadowy garden. She was entirely alone. With a sigh she pulled on her dress and wandered amongst the shrubs where she'd grown up as a child. Nothing had really changed there, but it all seemed different now, because she was seeing it through different eyes. It was the same with the house. In changing her Oliver had changed her memories. Her past seemed a distant blur. It was difficult to believe he'd been there for such a short time.

She wondered where her father was, and silently cursed him for deserting her. How could he have been so stupid as to gamble their family home away?

She couldn't get Jake's words out of her mind. It wasn't only the thought that she might eventually be handed over to him and Mary. He'd also reminded her that there would almost certainly be a life after Oliver, a more normal life, and she couldn't imagine how she was going to exist without the exotic pleasures her body now demanded.

Suddenly she pictured Christian's face. She knew he liked her, or at least desired her, and she wondered what life would be like with him. Would it be better? She guessed he would be less harsh, that there would be more consideration and less pain, but strangely that thought didn't please her as much as she would have expected.

'You took your time,' said Oliver, waiting for her when she finally reached her bedroom. 'You'd better have a little sleep before you bathe.'

'Do I have to wear something special?' she asked anxiously.

'It's a fairly formal dinner,' said Oliver. 'You'll be the most beautiful woman in the room.'

'You mean, I'll be wearing proper clothes?'

'Naturally. I want everyone to admire you. Mind you, you won't need any underwear.'

'But it's a proper dress?' persisted Selina.

Oliver raised an eyebrow. 'What a strange creature you are. You've been sitting outside, every inch of you exposed, our guests have touched you intimately, and yet still you worry about what you'll look like at dinner!'

'You don't understand,' murmured Selina.

'Of course I do. You feel more vulnerable when everyone else is looking elegant. You're frightened your lascivious search for carnal pleasure will show you up. Don't worry, that all comes later.'

Selina decided not to ask any more questions. Throwing herself on the bed she closed her eyes, and within a few minutes had fallen into a restless doze.

'Do you like it?' Oliver asked, holding up the outfit she was to wear that evening.

Selina, freshly showered and with her hair washed and shining, gazed at it in admiration. It was a cream-coloured two-piece, consisting of a full length straight skirt with a tiny slit at the back and a tight fitting jacket which flared out softly over her hips and had a rich lace trimming around the waist. The neck of the top was V-shaped, and she saw that there was a long matching scarf to go with the outfit.

'Nothing to say?' asked Oliver.

'It… it's beautiful,' said Selina, in awe. 'Thank you.'

'You need very little beneath it,' continued Oliver, ignoring her words of gratitude. 'I think cream hold-ups and some jewellery will suffice.'

'Jewellery?'

Oliver nodded. 'A present, from me to you,' he said, opening the bedside drawer. Selina was certain he was going to produce something really beautiful, but she was completely wrong. She should have known better. 'W-what on earth are those?' she asked in astonishment.

'Spread your legs,' he said.

She stared at the heavy diamond pendant hanging from a tiny chain that was attached to a small ring. 'My legs?'

'Of course. This precious stone is to adorn your most precious part.'

He crouched and peeled her sex lips apart, and then carefully started to arouse her a little until she felt her clitoris begin to swell. With a murmur of satisfaction he immediately imprisoned it with the ring, and she could feel a peculiar dragging heaviness.

'You can look in a moment,' he promised, and then stood up, the remaining jewellery in the palm of his hand.

'I… I don't want that on me,' she protested.

'But I want you to wear it, and that's what matters,' he

reminded her.

Selina stared hopelessly as he fastened two clips, one to each nipple. Hanging from each of the clips was a miniature handcuff charm linked with a chain, which hung provocatively between her breasts.

'There, now the jewellery is complete,' he said with satisfaction.

Selina felt the clips biting into her nipples and winced. 'These hurt,' she complained.

'You'll soon get used to them,' Oliver promised dismissively. 'Think how arousing it will be when they brush against your dress, or the chain catches against the fabric. Now, stand with your legs apart and look in the mirror.'

Selina stared at her reflection. With her legs parted the sparkling diamond hung down from between her sex lips.

'You'll be aware of it constantly,' said Oliver delightedly. 'It should prevent dinner from becoming too boring for you.'

The ring imprisoning her clitoris and the biting sensations of the nipple clips was exciting Selina already. Bending slightly, Oliver began to finger her casually between her thighs, almost contemptuously. 'You're very excited,' he said.

Selina felt the colour rising in her cheeks. 'Isn't that what you intended?' she asked.

'Yes, but the speed of your response still surprises and delights me. Now put on the clothes, it's time we went down.'

When they entered the dining room Selina noted the way the guests' eyes turned to them, and knew they were looking at her rather than Oliver. She wondered if they'd been expecting her to wear something more outrageous, more humiliating, but it was impossible to tell. If they were disappointed by what they saw, their faces gave no sign of it.

'How elegant you look,' said Christian, as he approached her with a drink. 'Oliver certainly knows class when he sees it.'

'Thank you,' said Oliver graciously.

'The compliment was intended for Selina,' retorted Christian, without taking his eyes from her.

She smiled hesitantly. 'You're very kind,' she said softly.

'Not always, but sometimes,' he said, with a polite nod of his head.

The meal lasted for a good few hours as the guests ate and drank their fill. Selina was careful not to consume too much, remembering what Oliver had told her when they were in London, and guessing that the same probably applied tonight. Besides, the butterflies fluttering in her stomach had all but killed off any appetite she may have had. She was anxiously preoccupied with whatever might lay in store for her. The prospect was chilling.

'Everybody,' Oliver suddenly called for attention when the desert bowls were empty and only scraps of cheese remained on the side plates. 'For the final part of the evening we have to go to the old wing of the house,' he announced, and Selina's stomach sank. 'There's a playroom and a dungeon there, which should ensure something for all. Naturally, Selina will be the focal point of our entertainment, but Georgina has very kindly offered Kim's services, should we require them. Please follow Georgina now, and she'll show you the way. I'll bring Selina along in just a few moments.'

'What's going to happen to me?' Selina asked Oliver when they were alone.

'Nothing particularly terrible. Nothing too different from what you've already experienced.'

'But why do these people need to be here?'

'Doesn't their presence excite you?'

Selina shivered. 'No, not really.'

Oliver massaged her shoulders, and she closed her eyes and sighed quietly.

'Oh, I think it does,' he said. 'I think you're a born exhibitionist, my dear.' His thumbs dug into tight muscles and she rolled her head appreciatively. 'This is your big night, Selina. It would hardly be a test if you'd done it all before.'

'And I'm free to leave if I want to?' she asked anxiously.

'Of course; that condition still applies. I've had Mary pack you a case. It'll be in the hall. If you do leave us I'd like you to be gone before we return here. We'll entertain ourselves with Kim to give you time to make your exit.'

'And if I succeed?' she asked. 'If I stay the course?'

Oliver's eyes were thoughtful. 'Then you may remain here. But I can't say what the future will hold.'

'You expect me to fail, don't you?'

'You'll be tested to the extreme,' he confirmed. 'If you do pass I'll know you have no limitations; that you're willing to trawl any depths in order to satisfy your carnal needs... and to please me.'

'Christian likes me,' Selina blurted, and immediately wished she hadn't.

Oliver's face darkened. 'Do you think I don't know that?'

'Well, doesn't that mean anything to you?' she asked, without really knowing why.

'I merely take it as a compliment.'

'I might leave you for him,' she pointed out, suddenly wanting to goad him.

Oliver shook his head. 'I doubt it. He would only offer a pale imitation of the life I've shown you. If you like what I've taught you, then you'll stay with me. If you don't, then you'll run away from us all. What would be the point of going to someone like Christian?'

'Perhaps he's more capable of caring for someone,' she suggested, hopefully.

'Perhaps he isn't as honest as me,' countered Oliver, harshly. 'Anyway, there's no point in discussing it. My guests will be waiting. It's time for us to go.'

Selina stood up, her hands smoothing down the skirt of her dress. 'Do… do you care for me at all?' she asked blankly.

'I don't know what you mean,' he said, and she suspected he was telling her the truth.

Selina took a deep breath and steeled herself, before saying bravely, 'Let's go then.'

Chapter Fourteen

True to Oliver's prediction, his guests were waiting eagerly as he guided Selina into the playroom.

Kim was there too. She was entirely naked, except for a tiny gold chain around her left ankle; a symbol of her servitude. Selina wanted to back away, but Oliver was right behind her, and there was no escaping his overpowering physical presence.

'I'll undress you,' he said, and with deft fingers he removed her elegant clothes, so that within seconds she stood timid and naked before the onlookers, her eyes closed to block them out.

'What a lovely diamond,' commented Harry.

Oliver flicked the heavy jewel with a finger, and Selina felt the tug on her clitoris as it swung to and fro.

'It'll have to come off now,' he said.

'The nipple clips look interesting, too,' purred Charlotte.

'Tell everyone what they've felt like, Selina,' Oliver prompted.

She hesitated for long seconds, and then whispered, 'They've kept me aroused.'

'Speak up,' he ordered sharply.

'They've kept me aroused,' she repeated instantly.

'And?'

'And my nipples ache,' she confessed. 'I can barely feel the tips any more, and yet every time the dress brushed against them I wanted...' she faltered.

'Wanted what?' he persisted relentlessly.

'I wanted to come,' she admitted, despairingly.

'Let's see what happens when I remove them,' continued Oliver, and Selina clenched her fists as the jagged teeth were at last pinched open and removed. She held her breath, and for a moment felt nothing at all. Then, as the circulation rushed back into her nipples she felt a delicious throbbing pain and squealed in confusion. She wanted to rub her tortured buds, to ease the discomfort and give herself pleasure, but her hands were slapped away.

'You'll get plenty of stimulation from us,' Oliver warned.

Standing so close, he could smell her sweet fragrance. She was glorious; a paradox of sensual innocence – confused and debased. He could have fucked her there and then. He allowed his stretched trouser-front to nudge gently against her bottom, and savoured her little intake of breath. She was giving him more satisfaction than any girl had ever given him before, and he genuinely hoped she wasn't going to fail him or lose her nerve now.

'I have a little present for you,' he said, reaching into his jacket pocket. He sensed her confusion as he produced what looked like a beaded necklace, and showed it to her. 'Do you like it?' he asked.

'It… it's very unusual,' she replied uncertainly.

'As you will notice,' he continued, 'it has no clasp. The knots at each end serve a very special purpose, though.'

Selina continued to look puzzled, and her exquisite naïvety made his cock strain all the more uncomfortably. He wondered how she was going to cope.

'Harry,' he said, turning his attention to his guest, and then indicating one of the wooden chairs, 'be so good as to position her over that, would you?'

Harry needed no second invitation.

Bent at the waist over the chair and with her legs spread, Selina looked timidly back over her shoulder at Oliver, and as he moved in he saw the understanding dawning in her eyes.

'No…' she whispered. 'Please… it's so humiliating.'

'But you'll enjoy it,' he soothed. Prising her buttocks apart he smoothed cold lubricating jelly, from a jar held for him by Georgina, between them and into the tiny puckered opening. 'Now, I'm going to feed these beads into you very slowly,' he explained patiently.

'Why are you doing this to me?' she pleaded softly.

'Because it is necessary,' was his only reply.

He nodded once, and upon his silent command the guests crowded in, hands holding her in position.

She protested no more, and so he positioned the first bead against her oiled anus, pressed a little, and then watched with approval as it popped inside. Her legs buckled a little, and a tiny smile lifted the corners of his mouth.

Bead by bead he fed the necklace into her bottom, and towards the end she began to moan in her shame. By the time he came to the last bead she was sobbing continually. Oliver straightened up and admired his handiwork; he gazed at her smooth buttocks and the tiny piece of string peeping out from between them.

Despite the intense humiliation Selina would be experiencing, he guessed she would be acutely turned on, and ran his fingers into her sopping sex to confirm his suspicions.

The mauling hands disappeared, and despite the weird sensations in her bottom, Selina struggled to ignore her excitement and her shame and straightened up. Leering faces watched her closely as she stood unsteadily, and used the back of the chair for some support. She sniffled a little and used the back of one hand to wipe the moisture from her eyes.

Suddenly Harry and Charlotte moved in again, gripped her arms, and held her firmly between them. Oliver took the protruding piece of string between finger and thumb, and slowly but steadily pulled the small balls out again. As the last one popped free Selina's head lolled forward and she shuddered with ecstasy between her two captors. The strange sensations and the acute chagrin had made her climax beautifully.

It was as much as Oliver could do to stop himself from releasing his bursting penis from its tight confines and forcing it into the clinging channel just vacated by the beads. It was so tempting, but the time was not right. Later perhaps, if she passed all the tests. Then he would indulge himself, but until then it was important that he wait and see if she really was the faithful submissive he judged her to be.

'You loved it, didn't you?' he accused, purposely increasing her shame before the gathered audience. 'You're insatiable.'

Selina couldn't meet his gaze. She kept her eyes lowered.

Oliver studied her for a moment, and compared the lovely creature who was still gently convulsing as her orgasm finally subsided, with the prim girl who'd opened the door to him on the night he'd arrived to claim Summerfield Hall as his own. The contrast was breathtakingly exciting, wickedly erotic, and he felt tremendous satisfaction at what he'd achieved in so short a time.

'I think we'll move on to the dungeon now,' he said, looking up at his spellbound guests. 'That's where our evening will end.'

Chapter Fifteen

Georgina watched Selina step unsteadily down into the gloomy dungeon. She looked extremely unsure of herself, and she looked enticingly vulnerable beneath the dim lighting and oppressive atmosphere so cleverly created by Oliver. She could imagine how Selina's heart would be pounding, and she licked her lips hungrily.

Georgina waited, whip in hand. This was her moment, her chance to see off the first girl who'd posed a real threat to her, and she didn't intend to fail now.

'The first thing you have to do, Selina,' said Oliver, calmly breaking the heavy silence once everyone was ready, 'is to ask Georgina to beat you.'

Georgina watched as Selina shook her head, clearly struggling to believe that Oliver could put her in such a situation. 'I… I can't,' she whispered.

Oliver's expression hardened. 'And why not?' he demanded.

'Because I'm afraid,' she implored. 'Because I couldn't stand it. You know that.'

Georgina was surprised that Selina was admitting to her weaknesses. It was a mistake, and would annoy Oliver.

'Don't whine,' he snapped, true to form. 'Either ask her to do it, or go.'

Selina looked across to where the blonde was standing. Georgina could imagine the tension and fear that would be engulfing the lovely girl, but knew she would be highly aroused as well. Georgina certainly was. She hadn't been so aroused for a long time, and could hardly wait to proceed.

Selina still looked bewildered, and Georgina knew she still didn't understand how she could have become the person she had; how she could take so much pleasure from her own pain and humiliation. They never did understand, and their confusion merely increased Georgina's enjoyment.

With a last despairing look at Oliver, Selina walked to Georgina and stood in front of her with her head bowed. 'P-please beat me,' she begged meekly.

Georgina was so excited that she felt perilously near to coming herself. It was wonderful to have Selina standing so submissively in front of her at last, just as she'd anticipated for some time. Slowly reaching out, savouring the moment, she grabbed the girl and pushed her roughly across to the beam where Jake had so recently hung.

Within a few minutes Selina was stretched up on tiptoe, her wrists shackled high to the beam and her taut muscles protesting as she revolved slightly and struggled to keep herself steady.

'Begin when you like,' said Oliver, with the air of a Roman emperor settling down for some entertainment.

Georgina prowled around Selina like a hunting cat, tapping the handle of the whip against her thigh, and occasionally cracking it through the musty air. Every time the leather hissed and spat Selina would jerk in fearful anticipation of the biting pain, and every time it failed to materialise Georgina could see Selina's desire heightening as her nipples stiffened. Georgina lazily felt between the suspended girl's thighs, and as she suspected, she was moist and ready.

For a long time Georgina kept the suspense building, until her trussed prey was muttering incoherently. Deciding the time was right, Georgina drew back her arm and the first blow swept into Selina's unprotected tummy, causing her to yelp with the shock and pain of it. Georgina shivered with delight, watching the girl twist and convulse like a marionette. She watched Selina's myriad of expressions very carefully, and just as she judged the moment was again right, she struck another blow beneath the first, and then soon the blows were raining down thick and fast on her opponent's fair skin.

It was clear to Georgina that unless she was careful Selina would orgasm very quickly, for despite her initial fear, the stimulation of the whipping was causing her breathing to quicken, and her arousal was evident. Determined to keep her waiting and to make her suffer as much as possible, Georgina lessened the strength of the blows whenever Selina's climax seemed imminent. Occasionally she would throw in a harder blow so that the pain totally overcame the pleasure, and she watched as Selina's orgasm receded and her features contorted with despair. After a short time Georgina lost count of the number of times the whip had fallen on the tormented body, but she knew Selina was desperate to come.

'Beg,' said Oliver from the murky shadows.

Georgina held her breath. This was the big test. Selina would understand what he meant, but Georgina didn't believe she could do what he wanted. In her experience, little innocents like Selina could never admit to their darkest needs – no matter what tortures they had to endure in the meantime.

As she waited she ran the tip of the whip up and down the straining sinews of her victim's curvaceous back, taking immense delight in the girl's ragged breathing and the sight of her frustrated and perspiring body, and proudly knowing her own expertise had induced such a condition.

Then, Georgina began to sense that she may have made a mistake and misjudged the girl. As she watched Selina slowly lifted her head, and there was a proud and triumphant sparkle in her eyes.

'Please,' she whispered hoarsely, 'let me come.'

Georgina couldn't believe that Selina had forced the words out, but she knew she had to comply with her wish. Cursing her costly miscalculation, she drew back her arm, and then with a swift flick of the wrist made the whip strike the top of Selina's shimmering breasts. At last the exhausted girl found the ecstatic relief she craved with a pulsating climax that had her writhing helplessly on the end of the chains.

When she was finally still, Selina and Georgina stared at each other, and the faintest of smiles played around Selina's pouting lips. With a sense of disbelief Georgina realised for the first time that in Selina Oliver might indeed have found his perfect partner. It was an unsettling realisation, and she turned away from the tethered girl, deciding to spend a few spiteful moments with Kim, to relieve her frustration and anger. She knew the weekend wasn't yet over, but her big opportunity had now passed, and Selina had managed to cope. All she could hope for now was that the others would be able to bring about Selina's downfall.

'Excellent,' said Oliver, with satisfaction. He moved in close to Selina and spoke to her, his voice a quiet monotone. 'You've done exceedingly well, so far. Better than I expected. Now, I'm going to hand you over to my friends for a while.' He looked at the eager group, already undressed and waiting for their moment of fun, before turning his attention back to the panting beauty. 'You'll not be tied down, so you'll be free to leave at any time you like. But if you can endure the next stage, you'll be very close to achieving your task.' He lifted Selina's chin, and looked into her tearful eyes. 'Do you understand me?'

The tiniest of nods told him what he needed to know, and

he smiled.

'Good,' he said, and then stepped back and addressed the watching group, which stood in the dingy orange light, almost salivating like a pack of starving animals.

'You may get her down and put her on there,' he said to them, pointing at the narrow cot that stood in the shadows of one corner of the dungeon. 'You will not need to bind her; I don't think she'll be resisting you in any way.'

Still shuddering slightly from the last moments of her climax, Selina was lifted by the fervent guests, carried to the cot, and laid down on her back. Many hands were touching as they positioned her as required. She felt like a doll, being manipulated to satisfy the lust of these depraved people. Surreptitious fingers took the opportunity to maul and grope, sliding between the cheeks of her bottom, into her wet vagina, or pinching and prodding her soft breasts and erect nipples.

Then the trespassing hands left her and there was an unsettling lull. Selina gingerly opened her eyes and peered up at the shadows looming over her, the faint light behind them. Their expressions were indistinct, but she knew what thoughts were in their heads. She filled her lungs deeply, her breasts rising in inadvertent invitation, and held her breath, awaiting the inevitable.

The cot squeaked slightly as Selina trembled. She desperately wanted to ask what was going to happen to her, to find out what the last test would be, but her lips suddenly felt dry and she was unable to utter a sound. In any case, deep down, she knew.

Then someone was speaking, and she realised it was again Oliver.

'My guests will now indulge themselves, Selina. They are free to do with your body as they wish: they may humiliate you, punish you, please you… anything within my express guidelines, of which they are well aware and of which there are few. As ever, you are free to call a halt to the proceedings at any time, but if you decide to leave me now, you will leave for good...'

There was another long and excruciating silence, and then, upon a signal which was unheard and unseen by the mesmerised girl, the shadows sank lower and smothered her as completely as a heavy blanket.

The intrusive hands returned, molesting and pulling and probing. Hot rasping breath and sweating flesh swamped her. Wet tongues lapped and wormed between her thighs and into her mouth. She became aware of a soft buzzing sound, and something vibrated beautifully against first one nipple, and then the other. She felt the tiny buds pucker in welcome to the delicious titillation. Then the vibrating moved into her cleavage, down her hollowed tummy, her sex was peeled open, and the bulbous plastic head was pushed deep into her body. Her back arched involuntarily, but the weight of her avaricious assailants kept her pinned to the hard cot. Fingers stroked her face and pumped suggestively in and out of her gasping mouth. Her legs were pulled further apart and her feet lifted, while her breasts were squeezed painfully until she squealed in delight and protest.

Selina had no idea who was doing what, and she didn't care. Her pleasure was building irresistibly until she feared she would drown beneath the heaving mass of male and female bodies.

A rigid column of flesh rubbed against her lips, and was then fed into her mouth until her nose was embedded in wiry hair and the swollen helmet nudged the back of her throat. Male scent invaded her nostrils as she breathed deeply, her breasts rising and swelling into the greedy hands that mauled them. The gnarled stalk pulsed against her tongue, and then it lurched violently and spat its seed deep into her throat. Selina swallowed gamely as her mouth filled again, and then the penis withdrew, leaving a viscous residue on her lips, which she savoured greedily with her tongue.

She was at the complete mercy of these decadent people, but begging for release didn't even enter her mind. Oliver was testing her resolve and her willingness to please him by obeying his wishes, and she had no intention of disappointing him.

Her wrists were gripped and lifted, and her fingers clamped to swaying breasts or guided between grinding buttocks. The dildo disappeared, and then pressed urgently against her rear entrance. A body slipped between her thighs, and as the dildo sank into her rectum it was mirrored by another erect cock which sank into her sex with one long slow lunge. Selina gasped, but her delirious moans were stifled as a soft breast was stuffed into her mouth. Lips closed around her nipples, and teeth pinched and chewed. She was in absolute heaven, and as the cock between her legs pumped back and forth and then erupted inside her, so she exploded into the most wondrous orgasm she had ever experienced.

Selina floated into a dreamlike state of undiluted ecstasy. Soon she'd lost count of the number of orgasms she'd had or the time that had passed. At one stage she was vaguely aware of being flipped over and her mouth being pulled into fragrantly juicy sex lips, as her buttocks were prised apart and another erection ploughed into her bottom.

She was pulled and twisted and contorted into numerous unimaginable positions. Orgasm after orgasm swamped her, and after a while her exhausted mind and body could take no more, and the last thing she remembered before drifting gratefully into unconsciousness was being screwed simultaneously by two rampant cocks and a monstrous vibrator...

Selina came round to find herself once again chained beneath the beam, the weight of her drained body pulling on her raised and bound wrists.

'What are we waiting for?' asked someone from the shadows. Selina lifted her eyes to the sound of the voice, and saw it was Jilly, her sweating body shimmering in the dull light.

'That's for Selina to decide,' said Oliver. He was standing before his trussed prize, naked, his erection spearing towards her from his dark groin.

Somebody else spoke. Selina moved her groggy head; it was Christian.

'You don't have to stay here,' he said softly. 'Don't say what he wants you to say. Come away with me – now. I'll be the perfect master for you.'

'But...' her mouth was dry, and she realised just how thirsty she was. 'But you don't know me,' she managed.

'Neither does he,' urged Christian. 'And he doesn't care either. You'd be happier with me, Selina. He's taught you all you need to know; you can't want to go any further. You're trained now; you'd make any man happy... except him. I'd demand nothing more of you than what you already know. Just say the word and we'll leave tonight.'

'Leave her alone,' said Oliver, arrogantly. 'Admit it, Christian, you've lost. Selina can decide for herself.'

'But I don't know what I'm supposed to decide!' she cried, and her throat was tight with unshed tears as her eyes beseeched Oliver to tell her what more he wanted of her, what more she could possibly do to show him that she was his. She'd submitted to everything; allowed him and his friends to use her in any way they liked. She'd even allowed Georgina to whip her, something she'd never dreamt he'd ask of her. And yet still there was something more; something she hadn't done, but needed to do in order to pass his final test.

'I'm waiting,' he said slowly.

Selina couldn't think. She was totally confused. Her body and soul no longer seemed her own, yet still he asked something more of her. She caught Georgina's eye; the woman was smiling, gloating at her lack of understanding. Her mind raced frantically as she tried to think what it could be, what the secret puzzle was she had to solve, because she knew now that she didn't want to go with Christian – it was Oliver she needed.

Georgina snorted derisively. 'You've done well with her Oliver, but I don't think she fully understands – even now.'

'Give her time,' said Oliver.

'How much time?' sneered Georgina. 'We could wait here until doomsday.'

'A few more minutes,' insisted Oliver.

Selina was growing desperate. What was she supposed to do or say? How long would she be kept suspended like a side of meat? Her eyes searched the faces of the debauched group for a clue, and then her gaze fell upon Kim, standing in the corner, hands tied behind her back, head bowed, a picture of submissiveness… and gradually it became clear.

Selina took a deep breath and lifted her head proudly. 'I'm… I'm sorry,' she said clearly.

Oliver stared at her. 'Repeat that,' he commanded.

'I'm sorry. I'm sorry I did wrong, and that you were forced to punish me.'

'And?' he persisted.

Selina swallowed hard. She knew now what she had to say. All that she needed was to summon the courage to somehow force the words out. 'And… and from now on I'm your slave… and I'd like you to punish me again,' she whispered. She managed to hold his piercing stare, and then, for the first time since she'd met him, Selina saw a genuine smile spread across Oliver's face.

'It will be my pleasure,' he said slowly as he advanced upon her. 'It seems you now understand the rules, and your station here.'

There remained a tense silence in the dank dungeon, but as soon as Oliver gripped her thighs and lifted them up around his waist, the heavy mood relaxed and the guests fell upon each other in a frenzy of entwined limbs. Even Christian seemed to have recovered from his disappointment, and was soon thrusting his erection into Jilly's mouth, his fingers buried in the kneeling female's hair.

Selina instinctively tightened her legs around Oliver's waist as he penetrated her, stretching her to the very limit, and she gloried in the fullness, the marvellous sensation of having him inside her. He thrust so deeply that the tip of his glans brushed against her cervix, and she whimpered in delighted surprise as a new kind of pleasure simmered there. It was a soft sweet ache, and she wanted it to grow, to spread throughout her body, and she heard herself crying out, urging him on.

Oliver needed no such instruction; he was lost in the sensations, his eyes staring deep into hers as he hurried towards his pinnacle of pleasure. 'You're not to come,' he gasped through gritted teeth. 'You're still being punished.'

Frustration overwhelmed Selina, for her own orgasm was all but upon her.

'Tomorrow morning,' he grunted, as his hips jerked back and forth, 'you will please each of my guests as they leave. Only then will your punishment be complete – and your submission total.'

Selina nodded weakly, determined to carry out Oliver's

order, because she needed him. She needed the perpetual arousal, the delayed gratification, and the dreadful pleasure-pain that he'd introduced her to. Without it her life would be totally empty. Even Christian no longer attracted her, because Christian lacked Oliver's need for absolute control. Selina was certain that she could never now be happy unless she was totally dominated, because through submission came freedom; freedom to allow herself to enjoy every kind of sexual excess and debauchery that was offered to her and, above all, freedom from guilt.

Chapter Sixteen

After breakfast the next morning Selina waited in the drawing room for the first of the departing guests to come to her.

The first were Harry and Charlotte. They clearly understood the game well, for Harry threw his wife onto the chaise longue, thrust into her for several minutes until they were both on the edge of orgasm, and then withdrew and gestured for Selina to kneel at his feet.

Swiftly she closed her mouth around his glistening cock, tasting his wife's juices on it as she sucked and licked, and within seconds he'd come, his hips jerking convulsively. Swallowing his sperm, she moved over to where Charlotte lay sprawled, legs apart, and used her mouth on her, licking and lapping until she found the most sensitive place. Again, within seconds, the woman was squirming, her body wracked by a short but intense orgasm. Once it was over neither of them spoke to her, but simply readjusted their clothing and left the room.

She had simply been a vessel for their pleasure, but in pleasuring them she felt proud; proud of her own sexuality and her ability to satisfy so completely in so many ways.

It took Georgina a long time to come, despite the fact that she'd ordered Selina to use a vibrating double dildo on her, and for a brief time Selina feared that she was going to fail. Eventually, however, Georgina's body quivered with ecstatic rapture and Selina hastily withdrew the vibrators, realising that even now it was important she didn't offend the blonde.

Georgina stood up and calmly straightened her clothing. 'You must be feeling very pleased with yourself,' she said coldly.

Selina was taken aback. 'Not really,' she said defiantly.

'I'm not misled by you,' continued Georgina. 'Oliver may think you're a sweet, naïve little thing, but I know better. You think that by submitting to him you've gained power over him, don't you?'

'No, of course not,' said Selina, but she knew there was more than a grain of truth in what the woman was saying.

'Well, you'll learn that you're wrong. I'll be interested to see how your little affair progresses. Don't imagine for one moment that you've seen the last of me, because you haven't. I don't believe you're right for Oliver. I don't think you're what he's looking for.

'And remember, when you visit London I shall be around to keep an eye on you. I'll be watching your every move, and as soon as you make a mistake...' she clicked her fingers to emphasise her point, 'that will be the end of it. You think the last few weeks have been difficult, but they've been nothing compared to what lies ahead now that you've chosen to stay with Oliver.'

'It's what I want,' Selina said stubbornly.

Georgina's eyes narrowed. 'But is it what's best for Oliver?' she hissed.

'Surely that's for him to choose,' insisted Selina, realising for the first time just how great an enemy she was acquiring by choosing to stay with Oliver. She didn't know why the woman was so vehemently opposed to their relationship, but she clearly was.

Georgina pointed a threatening finger at the kneeling girl. 'Just remember, you'll be seeing more of me from now on... a lot more.' And then she turned and stormed from the room in a swirl of elegant clothes and perfume.

The last guest to leave was Christian. He walked into the drawing room and looked at Selina with disappointment in his eyes.

'I've told Jilly to wait for me in the car, but I really thought you'd be leaving with me too,' he said, shaking his head with what appeared to be genuine sadness. 'I hate to lose to Oliver at the best of times, but particularly when losing to him means losing one as precious as you too.'

His touching display of sincerity unsettled Selina with a tiny seed of doubt. She tried to respond, but Christian continued.

'Tell me,' he said, 'why have you chosen to stay with the swine? You're far too good for him.'

Selina shook her head, a faint smile of irony playing around her lips as she pondered the fact that Georgina vehemently believed Oliver was too good for *her*. 'I'm too bad for you,' she murmured.

'That's not true,' said Christian. 'I could have made you happy.'

'No you couldn't,' she said confidently. 'No one could make me happier than Oliver.'

Christian shook his head. 'If you say so,' he said.

'I do.' She realised she really did feel something for Christian, but not enough to make her change her mind. 'Now, what would you like me to do for you before you leave?' she asked, smiling at him.

'I want nothing more from you, Selina,' he said kindly.

There was an awkward pause. They looked at each other in silence. Selina almost wavered... and then the door opened, and Oliver stood there.

'Finished?' he asked.

'I didn't expect to be interrupted,' said Christian, without taking his eyes from the beautiful girl.

'You seemed to be taking rather a long time.'

'What were you afraid of?' asked Christian. 'That we'd run off together. That you'd come in here and find the room empty?'

'It's time for you to go,' Oliver said curtly.

'I haven't given up,' Christian defiantly said to Selina, not caring that Oliver heard. 'I shall be back. One day you'll realise that you'll be better off with me.'

Oliver sighed. 'Don't you know when it's time to go?' he asked.

'I'm just leaving,' Christian assured him, and as Selina watched, he walked out of the room without a backward glance.

Oliver looked at Selina. 'Everyone said they had a wonderful time,' he said. 'And they said you were the perfect hostess.'

'I was well trained,' she replied.

'Did you enjoy the weekend?'

Selina thought for a moment. She remembered how the Saturday had begun, how she'd been led around on a leash, and the punishment that she'd endured in the stocks. She recalled the dinner and then the long night as she'd been tested to her limits. As she remembered, so her excitement grew, and she wriggled on the large chair. 'It was perfect,' she replied.

'I knew you'd enjoy it,' he said with satisfaction. 'Tell me what you'd like now.'

Selina looked up at him, certain that her need must be evident on her face. 'Isn't it obvious?' she asked.

'You have to say it,' he said firmly. 'You have to ask me.'

'I want to come myself,' she confessed.

'Tell me how you feel,' he ordered.

'I feel though I'm ready to explode,' she admitted. 'My nipples ache to be kissed and pinched, and I'm wet with need between my thighs.'

Oliver held out a hand. 'Then come with me,' he said. 'I'll soon make you forget Christian.'

Some hours later Oliver stood beside his bed, staring down at the sleeping figure of Selina. He'd never felt that way before. Never before had he met anyone able to submit herself so totally to his every desire, and to take genuine pleasure in whatever was inflicted upon her. She was perfect, the girl of his dreams, but he knew very well that their future together would be uncertain.

By her very nature, because of the skills he so admired, Selina was bound to attract others. Christian wanted her so badly that he hadn't been able to conceal it from Oliver, and normally Christian was as good at deception as Oliver himself. Oliver didn't underestimate Christian, he knew he would continue to try and take Selina away from him, and that if he wanted to keep her he must force her further and further into submission. She must become nothing more than an obedient sexual plaything, but at the same time she had to retain her own unique qualities.

Looking down on her now, her cheeks flushed, her hair tousled and her lips curling in a soft smile of satisfaction, he felt an unexpected desire to protect and cherish her. He was certain she needed him as much as he needed her, but she was endearingly flighty, and he sensed she could easily become bored or even led away by another. Already he was planning new things for her, new ways of tutoring that oh so eager and willing flesh, because there were things she had not yet done; depravities she had not yet witnessed or experienced with which he could excite and ensnare her.

As he stood gazing down, her eyes opened and she looked up at him, disorientated for a moment. 'What time is it?'

she asked sweetly, stretching.

Oliver shrugged. 'I've no idea.'

'What happens to us now?' she asked.

'We go to London,' he said decisively. 'There are new people for you to meet. New games to be played.'

'But have I passed the test?' she asked.

'It never ends.'

He was delighted to see a glint of excitement in her eyes as she smiled up at him, a startling cocktail of innocence and sensuality.

'I hoped you'd say that,' she sighed sexily. 'London will be wonderful.'

Oliver sat down on the bed, his hands automatically reaching for her tempting nipples. As his fingers closed around them and he watched her eyes widen with rising desire, he smiled at her. 'I agree,' he said. 'Now I want you to come.'

'Again?'

'Yes, and quickly,' he said, pinching harder, and he saw the flush of arousal spreading over her upper chest and neck, saw the pupils of her eyes dilate as the dark pain delighted her debased body.

'Come now,' he commanded urgently. Within seconds her pleasure was spilling over and she jerked helplessly on the bed, crying out in ecstasy, throwing back her head, and he was so excited by her obedience that he continued to squeeze the nipples until she came a second time.

Her spent body relaxed, and he pulled her to him and cuddled her head against his chest. 'Here's some champagne,' he said, handing her a sparkling crystal flute. 'To London, and the future.'

'To London,' she echoed, lifting the glass towards her lips. 'And to my next meeting with Christian,' she added, with a cheeky little grin.

Oliver stared at her in astonishment. Only then did he realise that possibly he'd underestimated her. Perhaps in the weeks and months that were to come he would be tested just as much as, if not more than, Selina herself. At first her temerity in goading him with his rival's name brought a surge of anger to his chest, but then he realised that he too was being offered a challenge, and for him a challenge was always irresistible. Slowly he tipped his glass, watching the champagne splash over Selina's body, running down the valley between her breasts and collecting in her navel, before trickling on down over her flat belly and shapely thighs.

'Lie back,' he said huskily. 'I'll drink from you.' And as his tongue began to lap at the fizzy bubbles he felt her hand lightly caress his thick hair, as though she too knew that the balance of power might just have shifted.

The suitcases were all packed. Jake, Mary and Mrs Soames had gone on ahead, and Selina stood waiting patiently for Oliver. She felt wonderful; more confident and alive than ever before, and as he came down the main staircase towards her she felt a glow of pride in the pit of her tummy. He'd taught her so much; made her the girl she was, and despite her submission she knew he was as trapped as she. In giving herself over to him so completely she had made herself indispensable, and she sensed that he would do anything in order to keep her.

As the luxury car cruised over the drive of Summerfield Hall, Selina glanced back at her home. 'How long before we return?' she asked.

'A few months, I would imagine. Although we might manage to get up here for the occasional weekend.'

'I'll miss it,' she said, with a pang of sadness.

'You'll be too busy to miss it,' he assured her.

'I suppose I will,' she said, a thrill of excitement churning with the sadness.

Inside her vagina she had the vibrating balls, and she saw Oliver's hand move to the remote control.

'I don't want you getting bored on the journey,' he remarked, and immediately they began to vibrate inside her, sparking instant desire.

'Suck me,' Oliver instructed, as he turned the car out onto the country lane. 'But you're not to come yourself. Not until we reach London.'

With a moan of delight Selina lowered her head, opened his trousers, and freed his waiting erection, offering a silent prayer of thanks to her father who had gambled away Summerfield Hall and inadvertently shown her such an incredibly exciting world, inhabited by Oliver and his friends. As her mouth closed around Oliver's purple glans and she tasted the delicious scent of him, she realised that she'd never been happier.

'You're not concentrating,' he snapped angrily, as he changed gear. Suddenly Selina's stomach tightened as she felt a moment's fear, and the fear was even more delicious than the arousal.

'I'm sorry,' she said submissively, and she heard Oliver sigh contentedly.